THE CHILDREN OF WILLOW FARM

Other titles by Enid Blyton in Armada

Adventures on Willow Farm
The Children of Cherry Tree Farm
Six Cousins at Mistletoe Farm
Six Cousins Again
The Rockingdown Mystery
The Ragamuffin Mystery
The Rubadub Mystery
The Ring O'Bells Mystery
The Rat-a-tat Mystery
The Secret Island
The Secret of Killimooin
The Secret Mountain
The Secret of Spiggy Holes
The Secret of Moon Castle
The Naughtiest Girl in the School
The Naughtiest Girl Again
The Naughtiest Girl is a Monitor
The Adventurous Four
The Adventurous Four Again
Mr. Galliano's Circus
Hurrah for the Circus!
Circus Days Again
Come to the Circus
Happy Day Stories
Six Bad Boys
The Put-Em-Rights
Those Dreadful Children
The Family at Red-Roofs
House-at-the-Corner
Storytime Book
Holiday House
Brownie Tales
Story Party

THE CHILDREN OF WILLOW FARM

ENID BLYTON

First published in Armada in 1975
by William Collins Sons & Co. Ltd.,
14 St. James's Place, London SW1A 1PF

Printed in Great Britain by
Love & Malcomson Ltd.,
Brighton Road, Redhill, Surrey.

CHAPTER I

GOODBYE TO LONDON!

ONE wild March day four excited children looked down from the windows of a tall London house, and watched three enormous vans draw slowly up in the square outside.

"There they are!" cried Rory. "They've come at last!"

"The moving has begun!" said Penny, jigging up and down beside the window-sill.

"Won't it be funny to see all our furniture going into those vans!" said Sheila.

"I shouldn't have thought that we would have needed *three* vans!" said Benjy, astonished.

"Oh, there are three more coming after these too," said Sheila. "Oh goodness—isn't it lovely to think we are going down to Willow Farm! A farm of our own! A farm as nice as Cherry Tree Farm."

"Nicer," said Benjy. "Much nicer. It's got more streams. And it's built on a hill so that we get a marvellous view, not down in a hollow like Cherry Tree Farm."

The four children were very happy indeed. The year before they had all been ill and had been sent for some months to live on their uncle's farm. The life had suited them well at Cherry Tree Farm, and all the children had grown strong and red-cheeked.

Then, when the time had come for them to return to their London home, their father had found that his business was bringing him in very little money—and Uncle Tim had suggested that he should put his money into Willow Farm, five miles away, and take up farming for his living.

The children's father had been brought up on a farm, and knew how to run one. The children, of course, had been mad with delight at the idea—and here it was, really coming true at last! They were all going to move into Willow Farm that very week!

It had taken three months to buy the place and arrange everything. Rory and Benjy, the two boys, had been to boarding-school, and had just returned home in time to move down with the girls, Sheila and Penny. Their mother had been very busy packing, and everyone had helped. It was such fun!

"I like London if we just come up for a pantomime or a circus," said Rory. "But the country is best to live in!"

"I'm simply longing to see Tammylan again," said Penny. "Oh, won't he be pleased to see us!"

Tammylan was a great friend of theirs. He was a strange man, who lived in a hillside cave in the winter months, and in a tree-house made of willow branches in the summer. He was called the "wild man" because he lived alone with animals and birds. Most people were afraid of him, but he was the children's greatest friend. He had taught them all about birds and animals of the countryside, and now they knew more about all the big and small creatures than any other children in the kingdom. It would be marvellous to see Tammylan again.

Mother put her head in at the door. "It's time for you to put your things on," she said. "Daddy will soon be bringing the car round. Say goodbye to all the nooks and crannies here that you have known since you were babies—for you won't be seeing them again!"

The family were going down by car, and the vans were following. Mother wanted to be ready for them when they came. The children looked at one another.

"I'm glad to be leaving here," said Benjy. "But we've had some good times in this tall old London house!"

He ran out of the room.

"Benjy's gone to say goodbye to the plane trees he can

see from his bedroom window!" said Rory. "He always loved those."

It was true. Benjy leaned out of his bedroom window and looked at the trees with their last year's balls hanging from bare boughs.

"Goodbye!" he said. "I've known you for eleven years, and you are nice all the year round! I like you now, with bare boughs. I like you when you are just leafing, with bright green leaves shining in the sun. I like you in the summer when you are thick and dark green. I like you in the autumn when you turn yellow and throw your leaves away. Goodbye, plane trees! I'm going where there are no plane trees, but willows, willows, willows all around, growing along the banks of silver streams!"

The plane trees rustled in the wind as if they were whispering back to Benjy. He drew in his head and suddenly felt a little sad. He would never forget those London trees—and he would always remember the little grey squirrels that sometimes ran up and down the branches.

Sheila went to say goodbye to every room in turn. "I don't want to forget anything," she said to Rory, who was with her. "I always want to remember our first home, though I am going to love our second home much much better. Goodbye, drawing-room—you look funny now with all the furniture just anyhow! Goodbye, study. I won't forget how often I've slipped down to you to take a book to read out of your bookcases! Goodbye, dining-room, I never liked you very much because you are so dark!"

Eight-year-old Penny stayed up in the nursery. That was the room she knew and loved the best. It was not called the nursery now, but was known as the schoolroom, because it was there that the two girls worked with their governess. Penny loved it.

She ran her fingers over the wallpaper, which showed a pattern of nursery rhymes. It had been repapered for Penny, four years before. She had chosen the paper herself. She knew every single person on it, every animal, every tree. How often she had looked at Jack and Jill always going up the hill, and how often she had wondered how there could possibly be room in the Old Woman's Shoe for all the children that were playing around it!

She opened the built-in toy cupboard and looked inside. It was empty now, for every toy had been packed in boxes. There were shelves there that had held trains and bricks and dolls.

"I wish you were coming with us, toy cupboard!" said Penny. "I've always loved you. It was always so exciting every morning to open your doors and see my toys looking at me again. And it has always been such fun to creep right inside you and shut the door and pretend I was a toy too!"

Penny was the baby of the family. Rory was a big boy now, fourteen years old, black-haired and brown-eyed. Sheila was thirteen, curly-haired and pretty. Benjy, dreamy old Benjy, who loved and understood all wild creatures so well, was two years younger—and then came Penny, three years behind him! She tried to be grown-up, so that the others would let her into their secrets and take her about with them, but it was sometimes rather difficult.

She looked round. She was quite alone. Rory and Sheila were saying goodbye to each room in turn. She could hear them in the spare-room now. Sheila was talking to Rory.

"Do you remember counting the cracks in the ceiling when we were both in here with measles? There's one crack over in that corner that looks exactly like a bear with horns—look, there it is."

Penny heard the two of them talking. She stared at the toy cupboard. Should she just get inside for the last time, and pretend she was a toy? Nobody would know.

She squashed herself in. It wasn't so easy now as it used to be, for Penny had grown. She shut the doors and peeped through the crack—and at once it seemed as if she was only three or four years old again!

"I'm a big doll, peeping through the crack in the door at the children playing in the nursery!" she said to herself. "What a funny feeling it is!"

Before she could get out again, Benjy came into the room. He looked round. Where were the others?

"Sheila! Rory!" he called. "Where are you? Penny!"

Penny didn't answer. She was too afraid of being called a baby to come out and show herself. She stayed as quiet as a mouse in the cupboard.

The other two came running in. They carried coats and hats for everyone. "Mother says we are to come at once," said Sheila. "Here are your things, Benjy. Where's Penny? Now wherever has she gone?"

Penny didn't move. She stared out through the crack. It was funny to see the others through the narrow chink. They looked different somehow.

The three children put on their coats. Mother came in.

"Are you ready?" she said. "Where's Penny?"

Nobody knew. "Oh dear!" said Mother. "Wherever can she have got to?"

Penny was suddenly afraid that everyone would go without her. She pushed open the doors of the toy cupboard and looked out. Benjy almost jumped out of his skin with surprise.

"I'm here," said Penny, in a small voice.

Everyone burst into laughter. They all knew Penny's old trick of getting into the toy cupboard and pretending to be a doll. Sheila was just going to call her a baby when she saw Penny's red face and stopped.

"Come along," she said, holding out her hand. "Daddy's waiting for us. Hurry, Penny!"

Penny squeezed herself out and put on her coat in silence. All the children went downstairs, their feet clattering loudly on the bare stairs. The house seemed suddenly strange and unfriendly. It would soon belong to somebody else.

They crowded into the car. Daddy and Mummy looked

up at the tall house, remembering many things. They had had happy times there. The children had grown up there. It was sad to leave—but how happy to be going to a lovely farmhouse set on a hill!

The engine of the car started up. They were off!

"Goodbye!" cried the children, waving to the old house. "We may perhaps call in and see you sometime in the future. Goodbye! We're off to Willow Farm, Willow Farm, Willow Farm!"

And off they went, purring through the London streets on their way to a new life down in the heart of the country.

CHAPTER II

WILLOW FARM

NOTHING is quite so exciting as moving house. Everything is strange and thrilling and upside-down. Stairs sound different. Meals are taken just anywhere, at all kinds of queer times. Furniture stands about in odd places. The windows are like staring eyes with no eye-brows, because the curtains are not yet up.

It was like that at Willow Farm when the family moved in. Penny thought it was too exciting for words. Everything was fun. It was fun rushing through the different counties to get to Willow Farm. It was fun to pass Cherry Tree Farm on the way and stop for a few minutes' chat with Uncle Tim and Auntie Bess.

"Wouldn't you like to get rid of the children for a few days and let them stay with us?" asked Aunt Bess. But for once the children did not smile at the idea of staying at their beloved Cherry Tree Farm.

They looked quite dismayed. Mother laughed. "Look at their faces!" she said. "No thank you, Bess dear—

they are all looking forward so much to settling in at Willow Farm. It is true that they will get in the way and be under my feet all the time—but . . ."

"Oh Mummy, we won't!" cried Penny. Then she saw the twinkle in her mother's eye and laughed.

"Aunt Bess, we love Cherry Tree Farm, but we wouldn't miss arriving at Willow Farm, our own farm, today, for worlds!" said Benjy.

"Have you seen Tammylan lately?" asked Rory.

"The wild man?" said Aunt Bess. "Yes—let me see, we saw him last week, didn't we? He wanted to know when you were coming, and said he would love to see you all again."

"Oh good," said Benjy, pleased. "He's got my pet squirrel for me. He's been keeping it for me while I was at school. I shall love to see Scamper again."

"Well, we mustn't stay longer," said their father. "Goodbye, Tim, goodbye, Bess. We'll come over sometime and let you know how things go."

Off they went through the lanes. The hedges were just beginning to leaf here and there. Celandines turned smiling polished faces up to the sun. Primroses sat in rosettes of green leaves. Spring was really beginning!

The car turned a corner and came in sight of a rounded hill. Glowing in the afternoon sun was an old farmhouse built of warm red bricks. It had a thatched roof, as had Cherry Tree Farm, and this shone a deep golden-brown colour, for it had been re-thatched for the new owners.

"Willow Farm!" shouted Rory, and he stood up in the car. "Willow Farm! Our farm!"

Benjy went red with pleasure. Sheila stared in silence. Penny gave little squeaks, one after the other. All the children gazed with pride and delight on their new home.

It was a lovely old place, three hundred years old, long and rambling, with queer tall chimneys, and brown beams that showed in the walls.

And there it was—the nicest farm in the whole world!

The windows were leaded, and there were green shutters outside each. The old front door was made of heavy brown oak, and had a curious little thatched porch above it, in which stood an old bench. Not far from the front door was the old well, rather like a Jack and Jill well. The water was not used now, but in the olden days there had been a bucket to let up and down.

Little gabled windows jutted from the thatch. The children stared up at them, wondering which windows belonged to their bedrooms. How lovely to peep out from those little windows in the early morning, and see the green fields and distant woods and silver streams!

Many streams flowed in and about Willow Farm. Along the banks grew the many many willows that gave the farm its pretty name. In the spring-time the pussy willows broke into gold when the catkins became the lovely golden palm. Other kinds of willows grew there too, and the bees murmured in them all day long later on in the spring-time.

"Daddy! Hurry up!" cried Rory. "Oh, let's get to the farm quickly!"

The car ran down a winding lane, with high hedges each side—then up on to the hillside beside a gurgling stream. Then into a big gateway, whose great wooden gates always stood open.

And there they were at the farmhouse door! Behind the farmhouse were the farm buildings—great barns with old old roofs, big sheds, stables and pens. The farmyard lay at the back too, and here the hens pecked about all day long.

The children tumbled out of the car in great excitement. They rushed to the door—but it was shut. Their father came to open it with a very large key. The children laughed to see it.

The door was thrown open and the children gazed into a large hall, with great beams in the rather low ceiling, and red, uneven tiles on the floor. Beyond lay open doors leading to the fine old kitchen and other rooms. How marvellous to explore them all while they were empty, and to arrange everything in them!

Everyone trooped in, chattering and exclaiming in delight. The place was spotless, for two village-women had been in to rub and scrub the whole week. The windows shone. The floors shone. The old oak cupboards, built into the walls, glowed with polish and age.

"Mummy! This farmhouse has such a happy, friendly feeling!" said Benjy, slipping his arm through his mother's. "People have been happy here. I can feel it."

So could they all. It was lovely to stand there and feel the happiness of the old house around them. It seemed glad to have them, glad to welcome them.

"Some houses have a horrid feeling in them," said Sheila. "I remember once going to see somebody in an old house down at the seaside, Mummy—and I was glad to come away. It made me feel unhappy. But other houses feel so content and friendly—like this one."

"Yes—I think people have loved Willow Farm very much, and have worked hard and been happy here," said their mother. "I hope we shall work hard too and be happy. It takes a lot of time and hard work to make a farm pay, you know, children. We must all do our bit."

"Of course!" said Rory. "I'm going to work like anything! I learnt quite a lot on Uncle's farm last year, I can tell you!"

"Let's go all over the house!" said Penny running to the stairs. They ran up to a wide landing. There were seven rooms upstairs, one fine big room that their mother and father were going to have, one big room for the children's own playroom, a small room for Rory, a tiny one for Benjy, a bigger one for the two girls, a spare-room for friends, and a room for Harriet, the cook, who was coming in the next day.

And over the bedrooms was a queer attic, right under the thatch itself. It was reached by a funny iron ladder that slid up and down. The children went up it in excitement.

"Oooh!" said Penny, when she saw the dark cobwebby loft. "It smells queer. Oh look—this is the thatch itself. Put your torch on, Rory—have you got it?"

Rory had. He took it out of his pocket and switched it on. The children gazed round the loft. They could only stand upright where the roof arched. They touched the thatch. It was made of straw. There was nothing between them and the sky but the thick straw—no plaster, no tiles—just the straw.

"The thatcher hasn't finished thatching the kitchen end of the house," said Sheila. "I heard Daddy say so. We'll be able to see exactly how he does it. Isn't it fun to be going to live in a thatched house? We shall be lovely and warm in the winter-time!"

The children climbed down the loft ladder. Rory slid it back into place.

"I do like all these black beams," he said, looking round. "I think they look exciting. Daddy says they came from old wooden ships. When the ships were broken up, the beams were used in houses—so once upon a time all the wooden part of Willow Farm was sailing on the sea!"

"I like to think that," said Benjy, touching the black oak beam near him. "Funny old beam—once you knew the fishes in the sea, and you creaked as great waves splashed over you. Now you live in a house, and listen to people's feet going up and down the stairs."

The others laughed. "You do say odd things, Benjy," said Rory. "Come on—let's go down. I want to see the rooms below too."

Down they went. The big dark hall they had already seen. There was a large room that Mummy said would be a lounge or living-room. It had an enormous stone fireplace. Rory looked up it. He could stand on the hearth and look right up the chimney, and see the sky at the top. It was really enormous.

"I could climb up this chimney!" said Rory in surprise.

"Little boys used to," said Daddy, with a laugh. "Yes—you may well stare. It's quite true. In the days when most houses had these big fireplaces and chimneys, little boys used to be forced to go up them to sweep them."

"I do wish I could climb up and sweep it when it needs it," said Rory, longingly.

"You might want to do it for fun, but you wouldn't want to do it every day of your life!" said his father.

The children went into the next room. It was a long dining-room, panelled with oak. "I wonder if there are any sliding panels!" said Benjy, at once. He loved reading stories of hidden treasure, and in the last one he had read there had been a most exciting sliding panel, behind which a safe had been hidden.

"The one over there by the door looks as if it might slide!" said his father. Benjy stared at it. Yes—it really didn't seem to fit quite as well as the others. It *might* slide back! In great excitement he tried it.

And it did slide back! Very silently, very neatly it slid back behind the next panel. Benjy gave a yell.

"Daddy! Look!"

And then everyone laughed—for behind the sliding panel were four electric light switches! The people who had lived at Willow Farm before had hidden their switches there, rather than spoil the look of the panelling by the door! So poor Benjy didn't find hidden treasure or anything exciting.

The kitchen was a very big room indeed, with plenty of leaded windows, opening on to the farmyard at the back It had an enormous door that swung open with a creak. The sinking sun streamed through it.

"It's got the biggest fireplace of all!" said Sheila.

"Yes—many a fine meal has been cooked there!" said

her father. "And look here—at the side is a funny bread-oven, going right into the thick wall. Harriet will be able to bake her bread there!"

"I like the uneven floor," said Penny, dancing about over it. "All these nice red tiles, higgledy-piggledy. And I like the great old beams across the ceiling. Just look at all the hooks and nails, Mummy!"

Everyone gazed up at the big beams, and saw the rows of hooks and nails there.

"That is where people have hung up hams and onions, herbs and spices," said Mummy. "It's a shame to see all the kitchen beams empty and bare—but never mind, soon Harriet will use them, and then our kitchen will look a most exciting place!"

Off the kitchen was a great cool room with stone shelves—the dairy. Here the milk was set for cream to form, and the eggs were washed, graded and counted. The butter-churn was there too. All the children tried their hands at it.

"Oh Mummy! Won't it be fun to bring in the eggs and sort them, and to make the butter, and see the cream coming on the big bowls of milk!" cried Penny. She danced about again and fell over an uneven tile in the floor.

"Well, it's a good thing you weren't carrying eggs just at that moment!" said Sheila. "That would have been the end of them!"

There was just one more room downstairs—a tiny cubby-hole of a room, panelled in black oak—and Daddy said that was to be his study and nobody was to use it except himself.

"Here I shall keep my accounts and find out if Willow Farm is paying or not!" he said.

"Of *course* it will pay!" cried Rory.

"Farming isn't so easy as all that," said his father. "You wait and see!"

CHAPTER III

A LITTLE EXPLORING

JUST then the children heard a rumbling noise outside and they rushed to the window.

"It's the first van!" yelled Rory. "Look there it comes—in at the gates. Goodness, there's only just room!"

"That's good," said Mummy, pleased. "Only one van is arriving tonight—this one. It has our beds and bedding in, so that we can make do for the night. The others come first thing tomorrow."

The great van rumbled up to the door. The back was let down, and soon the children were watching four men carrying their beds, mattresses, pillows and everything into the house.

"You're in the way, children," their mother said at last, after Penny had nearly been knocked over by the end of somebody's bed. "Go and explore the farm, there's good children. Surely you want to see what it's like! You've seen the house from top to bottom—now go and see if you like the farmyard and the barns and the sheds!"

"Oh yes!" cried Rory. "Come on, all of you. Let's explore the back, where the barns are."

Off they rushed, munching large slices of cake, which their mother had given them. The farmyard at the back was rather exciting. It was a big squarish place, surrounded by sheds and stables. No hens pecked or clucked there. Those were to come. No pigs looked out of the sty. No cattle stamped in the sheds, and no horses looked out of the stable-doors.

"Uncle Tim has promised to buy all we want," said Rory. "I say—won't it be gorgeous when we've got hens and ducks all over the place, just like we had at Cherry Tree Farm? I miss the cackling and clucking, don't you? Look—there's the duck-pond over there."

The children looked. Through a field-gate gleamed a round pond, set with rushes at one end. Willow trees drooped over it. A moorhen swam across the water, its head bobbing to and fro like a clockwork bird's!

The children peeped into the big barn. It was so large that it seemed almost like a church to them. It was dark and peaceful. Much hard work had been done there. Men and women had laboured from dawn to dusk, had been tired and happy, and the old barn seemed to be dreaming of those long-ago days as the children walked inside.

It was tiled in dark red tiles, and green and yellow moss grew thickly over the roof. Some of the tiles were missing, and the daylight came in through the holes.

"We shall have to see that the roof is mended," said Rory, solemnly. "Uncle Tim always said that a good farmer looks every day at his roofs, gates and fences. He said that a nail in time saves nine, and a tile in time saves a hundred!"

"Well, it will be fun to go round each day and look at everything," said Benjy. "I say, look—are those our sheep up there on the hill?"

Everyone looked. There were about fifty sheep dotted about on the hillside—and with them were many little lambs. In a sheltered place, tucked away behind a copse of trees, was the shepherd's hut. The shepherd stood outside, looking up to the sky.

"We've got a shepherd—look!" said Rory. "I wonder if he's as nice as Uncle Tim's at Cherry Tree Farm? Shall we go and talk to him today—or shall we explore all the rest of the out-buildings?"

"Oh, let's explore," said Penny. "I want to see the cow-sheds—I always like the smell of those."

So into the empty sheds they went, where the sweetish smell of cows still hung. They ran into the stables and pulled at the hay still left in the stalls. They went into the little barn, where a wooden ladder ran straight up to lofts above.

They all climbed the ladder. A few husks of wheat blew about the floor. The loft had been used as a storing place for many years. In another loft nearby were a few old rotten apples.

"Oh—this is where they used to put the apples," said Sheila. "I say—won't it be fun to pick the apples in the autumn, and the pears too, and bring them up here to store away!"

"Doesn't it smell nice!" said Penny, sniffing the loft. "Years and years and years of apples I can smell!"

The others laughed. "Let's go to the orchard now and see what we can find there," said Sheila. "Auntie Bess said that Willow Farm had fine fruit trees. Come on!"

Down the steep wooden ladder they went. Rory held out his hand to help Penny, as she scrambled down too—but she would not take his hand.

"I wish you wouldn't think I'm still a baby," she said crossly. "I can get up and down ladders just as well as you can!"

She fell over a stick in the yard and Rory laughed. He helped her up. "You're not a baby," he said, "but you're a little goose at times. A gosling! I say—I wonder if we shall keep geese."

"Aren't they rather hissy?" asked Penny, remembering an alarming walk one day when she had come across a line of hissing geese who had looked at her quite fiercely.

"Very hissy and very cackly," said Rory, solemnly. "You'll have to take my hand every time you go past them, little gosling!"

Penny tried to look cross, but she couldn't. She skipped along in front of the others to a big gate that led into the orchard. It was a really lovely place.

Daffodils were in bloom beneath the fruit trees. They nodded and danced in the pale evening sun. Penny picked a bunch to take back to her mother.

"What fruit trees are these?" asked Sheila, looking down the straight rows.

"Apples—pears—plums," said Rory, who was quite good at telling one tree from another. "And oh look—those must be cherries in the next field! They are all bursting into bud! They will be heavenly in a week or two. Golly! What fun we shall have in the fruit-picking season!"

They wandered through the orchard, where hundreds of daffodils danced to them. They came to a little stream, whose banks were set with yellow primroses. A moorhen looked at them from some rushes nearby and then ran away.

"Moorhens always seem to be running away," said Penny. "I'd like to see one close. Rory, will the moorhens nest on our farm, do you think? I'd so like to see a whole crowd of black babies going along behind their mother. Do you remember Tammylan showing us a nest once, and we saw all the babies tumbling out into the water to hide themselves?"

The mention of Tammylan made the children remember him and long to see him.

"We *must* see old Tammylan tomorrow!" said Benjy. "And I *must* get back my squirrel Scamper!"

Tammylan had given Benjy the squirrel for his last birthday. Scamper had been a tiny baby squirrel when Benjy had first had him—now he was full-grown and the boy longed to see him. He had given Scamper back to Tammylan in the New Year, because he had not been allowed to take the squirrel to school with him—and Tammylan had promised to take great care of him.

"We shall be nearer to Tammylan's cave here than we were at Cherry Tree Farm," said Rory, pleased. "We can take the short cut over Christmas Common, and then down into the valley where Tammylan lives. That's good. Maybe he will help us a bit with the farm too. He knows such a lot about everything."

"Dear old Tammylan," said Benjy. "We've had some good times with him—we made friends with nearly every creature of the countryside because of him!"

A bell rang loudly from the farmhouse. The children turned. "That's Mummy," said Penny. "She wants us back. Well, that cake was good—but I'm hungry all over again now—and I'm getting cold too. Oh, what a lovely place Willow Farm is—aren't we lucky to come and live here!"

"We jolly well are!" said Benjy. "Come on—let's go this way. It leads through the farmhouse garden. Mother says she is going to grow her flowers there, and her herbs. And look—through that white gate is the soft fruit—the gooseberry bushes, the currants—raspberries and strawberries. Mummy will be kept busy making jam, won't she?"

"Oooh! I shall help her with that," said Penny, at once, thinking with joy of great fat red strawberries and sweet raspberries.

"I shouldn't like you to help *me* with jam-making!" said Sheila. "I know what would happen to all the fruit. There wouldn't be much left for jam!"

Penny laughed. She felt very happy. Her legs were tired now and would not skip. She walked along beside the others and suddenly yawned loudly.

"Now Penny, for goodness sake don't start yawning," said Benjy. "We shall all be sent off to bed at once if you do. That's just like you!"

"Sorry," said Penny. "I promise I won't yawn when I get indoors. It's awful the way grown-ups always seem to think you are tired out as soon as you do even the tiniest yawn. My mouth sometimes really aches with trying not to yawn."

"Well, you let it ache tonight," said Rory. "The first

evening in a new home is far too exciting to be spoilt by being sent off to bed because of a yawn!"

They clattered into the farmyard. The big kitchen door stood wide open. A pleasant noise of crackling wood came to the children's ears as soon as they opened the door.

Their mother had decided to use the kitchen that night, and she had lit a fire in the big hearth. She had thrown on heaps of dry wood, and the fire crackled merrily, lighting up the kitchen gaily. Shadows danced and flickered. It was fun to come in and see such a fine fire. The kettle boiled on a stove nearby, and the big old farmhouse table, which had been bought with the house, was spread with a cloth.

The children's father lit some candles, which he stood on the table and on the mantelpiece. The electric current had not yet been switched on. Everyone was to have candles until proper shades and lanterns were bought. The children all thought that candles were much nicer than anything. Even Penny was told she was old enough to have one to take upstairs. She had been rather afraid that her mother would think her too little.

The children looked at the table. There were loaves of white and brown bread, home-made jam given to them by Aunt Bess, a big currant cake, a jar of potted meat, and a big jug for hot cocoa. It looked good to them!

"There are no chairs yet," said their mother. "Take what you want and go and eat it sitting on the broad window-sills."

So the children spread their bread with butter, and with potted meat or jam, and then took their slices to eat on the window-sill. It was lovely to sit there, looking out at the darkening fields, or into the big, friendly kitchen, and see the leaping flames of the log-fire. The candles burned steadily, but the shadows jumped about the kitchen as if they were alive.

"This is nice," said Penny, in a dreamy voice. "I feel

as if I'm asleep and dreaming some lovely dream. I feel . . ."

Rory gave her such a nudge that she nearly fell off the window-sill. She glared at him. "Why did you . . ." she began.

"You *would* start talking about being asleep and dreaming, just to make Mummy think we are all tired out!" said Rory, in a low, fierce voice. Then he spoke in his usual loud clear voice. "May I have a slice of cake, please?"

"Come and get it," said his mother, cutting him a large slice. "Aren't you tired, Rory? You've had a long day, all of you."

"*Tired!*" said Rory, as if he had never in his life heard the word before. "*Tired!* Why should any of us be tired, Mummy? Gracious, I'm so wide awake that I could go and milk the cows or count the sheep or fetch in eggs!"

"Well, we won't ask you to do any of those things, Rory," said his father, with a chuckle. "If anyone is tired, it's your mother! She has made all your beds—they are ready for the night."

"Yes—and I really think I'm just about ready for mine," said Mummy, unexpectedly. "I feel as if I've done ten days' work in one. I've loved it all—and tomorrow will be fun, welcoming the other vans and arranging all the furniture. But I do feel I'd better have a long night, or I shan't be able to do a thing tomorrow."

"Oh Mummy—do you mean to say we've all got to go to bed?" said Penny in dismay. "And I've been trying so hard not to yawn!"

Everybody laughed at Penny's face. Then Mummy yawned. She put up her hand but there was no hiding it—and at once everyone else yawned too. They were all tired—and it was lovely to be able to yawn and feel that bedtime was not far away after all!

"As a matter of fact I'm really looking forward to going to bed," said Sheila. "I keep thinking of that nice room

Penny and I are sharing together. It will be so cosy at night."

"And I keep thinking of my own tiny room, with its slanting ceiling, and jutting-out window," said Benjy. "Mummy, can I shut the shutters?"

"Certainly not," said his mother. "You must get in all the air you can, silly boy, not shut it out. We shall only use the shutters for show—unless a tremendous storm comes and we put up the shutters to keep the wind out."

"Oooh—I hope that happens," said Penny, imagining a most terrific storm battering against the windows. Then she yawned again—so widely that Rory wondered how she could manage to make her small mouth so big! Then all the children yawned loudly at once, and their mother got up.

"Light your candles and off to bed, all of you!" she said. "I'll just wash up—and then I shall go too."

The children lit their candles. It was fun. Their mother said she would look in and say goodnight to them, so they kissed their father goodnight and went up the old stairs one by one. The candles flickered as they went. The old house seemed peaceful and friendly as they clattered up the stairs. Willow Farm! They were living there at last. It seemed too good to be true.

They went to their rooms. Their beds were put up, and covers turned down. Their night-dresses and pyjamas were ready. Their tooth-brushes were in the bathroom so one by one they went to wash and clean their teeth.

"After all, I *am* tired," said Benjy, as he turned in at the door of his own little room. "I don't believe I could have kept awake very long!"

They all said goodnight. The two girls went to the room they shared, and each got into her own little bed. Rory had the room next door. They heard his bed creak as he got into it.

"Goodnight!" he yelled. "Won't it be fun to wake up

at Willow Farm tomorrow morning! I guess I shan't know where I am for a minute or two."

"Goodnight!" called Benjy. "Tomorrow we'll go and see old Tammylan. Good old Tammylan!"

Then there was silence—and when the children's mother came up in ten minutes' time, she couldn't say goodnight—because every single child was fast asleep!

CHAPTER IV

THE FIRST DAY

BENJY awoke first the next morning. The sun came in at his window, and when he opened his eyes he saw a golden pattern of sunlight on the wall. He remembered at once where he was, and sat up in delight.

"It's our first real day at Willow Farm!" he thought. "I shall see Tammylan today—and Scamper. I wonder if Rory is awake."

He slipped into Rory's room, but Rory was still fast asleep. So Benjy put on his clothes and went downstairs all by himself. He let himself out into the farmyard through the big kitchen door. The early morning sun was pale and had little warmth in it, but it was lovely to see it.

"I wish there were hens and ducks clucking and quacking," thought Benjy. "But there soon will be. My word, how the birds are singing!"

The early morning chorus sounded loudly about Benjy's ears as he wandered round the farm. The chaffinches carolled merrily—"chip-chip-chip-cherry-erry-erry, chippy-ooEEEar!" they sang madly. Benjy whistled the song after them.

Blackbirds were sitting at the tops of trees singing

slowly and solemnly to themselves, listening to their own tunes. Thrushes sang joyfully, repeating their musical sentences over and over again.

"Ju-dee, Ju-dee, Ju-dee!" sang one thrush.

"Mind how you do it, mind how you do it!" called another as Benjy jumped over a puddle and splashed himself. The boy laughed.

"Soon the swallows will be back," he thought. "I wonder if they'll build in the barn. It will be lovely if they do. After all, their real name is barn-swallow—and we have lots of barns. I must peep in and see if I can spy any old nests."

It was too dark in the barn to see if the remains of old swallows' nests were on the rafters high in the roof. But Benjy saw the old nests of house-martins against the walls of the farmhouse. Two or three were just below his own window!

"I say—how lovely if they come back next month and build again there," thought Benjy, gazing up at his little jutting-out window, tucked so cosily into the thatch. "I shall hear their pretty twittering, and see the baby martins peeping out of the mud-nests. I hope they come back soon."

Far in the distance the shepherd moved in the fields. He was doing something to one of the sheep. Nobody else seemed to be about at all. There were no animals or birds to see to, nothing to feed.

But wait—somebody *was* about! Benjy saw the end of a ladder suddenly appearing round the corner of the farmhouse. Who could be carrying it?

A man came round the corner, whistling softly. He saw Benjy and stopped.

"Good morning, young sir," he said.

"Good morning," said Benjy. "Who are you?"

"I'm Bill the thatcher," said the man. "I'm just thatching the house for you—and after that I'm going to take a hand on the farm to get you all going!"

"Oh, that's fine!" said Benjy, pleased, for he liked the look of the man very much. His face was burnt as brown as an oak-apple, and his eyes were like bits of blue china in his brown face. They twinkled all the time.

Bill took the ladder to the kitchen end of the farm-house. Lying on the ground nearby was a great heap of straw.

"I do wish I could thatch a roof," said Benjy. "You know, we learn all sorts of things at school, Bill—like what happened at the battle of Crecy and things like that—and yet nobody thinks of teaching us how to do really useful and exciting things like thatching a roof. Think how good it would be if I could say to my father—'Let *me* thatch the roof, Daddy!' Or 'Let *me* clean out the duck-pond!' Or, 'Let *me* sweep the chimney!' "

Bill laughed. "Well, you come and watch me do a bit of thatching," he said. "Then maybe next year when the old summer-house over there wants patching up with straw, you'll be able to do it yourself!"

Bill had a great many willow-sticks that he had cut on his way to Willow Farm that morning. He began to cut them into short strips and to sharpen the ends. Benjy watched him. "What do you want those for?" he asked.

"To peg down the straw thatch near the edge, young sir," said Bill. "Look and see the piece I've finished."

Benjy looked, and saw that the thatcher had made a very neat edging near the bottom of the thatched roof. "It looks rather like an embroidered pattern!" he said. "Do you put it there just to look pretty?"

"Oh no," said the thatcher. "The straw would work loose if it wasn't held towards the bottom like that—but the pattern is one used by many thatchers. My father used it, and his father before him. Look at the top of the roof too—see the pattern there? Ah, thatching isn't so easy as it looks—it's a job that goes in families and has to be learnt when you're a boy."

"Oh good," said Benjy, glad that he was still a boy and

could learn to thatch. "I say, do you think you'd just wait till I call the others? They'd loved to see you do the thatching."

"You go and get the others, but I'll not wait," said the thatcher going up the ladder with a heavy load of straw on his shoulder. "A minute here and a minute there—that's no use when you've work to do. I don't wait about. I'll be at work all day and you'll have plenty of time to see me."

At that moment the other three came out. They saw Benjy and rushed at him. "Why didn't you wake us, you mean thing? You've been up ages, haven't you?"

"Ages," said Benjy. "Everything's lovely! Look—that's the thatcher. His name's Bill. See those willow-twigs he's been sharpening—they're for making that fine pattern to hold down the straw at the edges of the roof."

"You *have* been learning a lot!" said Rory, with a laugh. "Tell us how a roof is thatched, Benjy!"

"Well," said Benjy, making it all up quickly in his head, "the thatcher pulls off all the straw first—and then he . . ."

The thatcher gave a shout of laughter. Benjy stared at him. "What's the matter?" he asked.

"I'd just like to set you to work thatching!" he chuckled. "My you'd give yourself a job! Now look what I do—I pull out about six or seven inches of this old rotten straw—see—and work in handfuls of the new—about twelve inches thick. That'll work down flatter when the rain comes. You don't need to pull off all the old straw—that would be a real waste. When a roof is re-thatched we just pull out what's no use and pack in the new."

"Do you mean to say then, that there is straw in our roof that may have been there for years and years and years?" asked Rory, in surprise.

"Maybe," said the thatcher, with a grin, as he swiftly pulled and pushed with his strong hands, working in the new straw deftly and surely. "Ah, and you'd be surprised the things I've found hidden in old thatch—boxes of old coins, bits of stolen jewellery, bags of rubbish—a thatched roof was a favourite hiding-place in the old days."

The children stared at him, open-mouthed. This was marvellous! "Did you find anything in *our* thatch?" asked Penny hopefully.

"Not a thing," said Bill. "It's the third time I've thatched and patched this roof—I don't reckon I'll find anything this time if I didn't find it the first time! Now look—isn't that somebody calling you?"

It was the children's father, looking for them to come to breakfast. They left the thatcher and hurried indoors, full of what Bill had said. Penny thought it must be the most exciting thing in the world to be somebody who might at any moment find treasure in a roof. She made up her mind to go up into the loft above her bedroom and poke about in the thatch there. She might find something that the thatcher had missed!

"You must get out of our way this morning," said their mother, as they finished up their breakfast with bread and marmalade. "The other vans are coming and we shall be very busy."

"Oh—can't we stay and help?" said Benjy, disappointed. "I do like seeing the furniture being carried up the stairs, Mummy."

"Well, the men don't feel quite so excited about that as you," said Mummy. "No—I shall make you up a picnic lunch—and you can go and find Tammylan!"

There were loud cheers then! Everyone wanted to see Tammylan.

"Good," said Benjy, pleased. "I'd like that better than anything. And it will be fun to come back and see all the rooms with their furniture in, looking so nice and homey."

"Oh, you won't find that yet!" said his mother, laughing. "It will be a week or two before we are straight. Now, what would you like for your picnic lunch, I wonder?

I'll make you some potted meat sandwiches, and you can take some cake and a packet of biscuits. There is a big bottle of milk between you too, if you like."

Before they started off to find Tammylan the girls made the beds and the boys helped to wash up and to cut the sandwiches. Just as they were packing the things into two bags for the boys to carry, there came the rumbling of the big removal vans up the lane.

"Just in time," said their mother, running to the door. "Now we shall be able to get rid of you children for a while whilst the men unload!"

The children got their hats and coats and went outside the big front door. The first van drew up outside and the men jumped down. They opened the doors at the back and the children gazed inside and saw all the furniture they knew so well.

"There's the nursery table!" yelled Penny.

"And there's the old bookcase," said Rory. "I suppose Mummy has got to tell the men which room everything's to go into. I half wish we could stop and help."

"Go along now!" cried his mother. "Don't wait about there in the cold!"

The children set off, looking behind every now and again. They decided to go over the top of Willow Hill and across Christmas Common to Tammylan's cave. It was about two miles away. When they reached the top of the hill they looked down at Willow Farm. It stood firmly in the hillside, smoke curling up from the kitchen chimney. It looked alive now, with people running about and smoke coming from the chimney.

Then over the hill went the four children on their way to old Tammylan. They sang as they went, for they were happy. It was holiday time. The spring and summer were coming. They had a home in the country instead of in London. And Tammylan could be seen as often as they liked! They had missed him so much.

They rounded a small hill. Bracken and heather grew

there, and birch trees waved lacy twigs in the wind. The children made their way to a spot they knew well.

It was a cave in the hillside. In the summer-time tall fronds of green bracken hid the entrance, but now only the broken, russet-brown remains of last year's bracken showed. The new bracken had not even begun growing. Heather dropped its big tufts from the top edge of the cave.

The children stood outside and called. "Tammylan! Tammylan!"

"Let's go inside," said Rory. "I'm sure he's not there—but he *might* be asleep!"

"Don't be silly!" said Benjy, scornfully. "Why, old Tammylan wakes if a mouse sits up and washes his whiskers! He would have heard us coming round the hill long ago if he'd been here."

They went into the cave. It was exciting to be back there again. It opened out widely inside. The ceiling rose high, dark and rocky.

"Here's his bed," said Rory, sitting down on a rocky ledge, on which Tammylan had put layers of heather and bracken. "And look—he still keeps his tin plates and things on the same shelf."

The children looked at the little rocky shelf opposite the bed. On it, clean and neatly arranged, were Tammylan's few possessions.

"There is the stool that Rory and I made for Tammylan for Christmas!" said Benjy, in delight. "Look—see the squirrels I carved round the edge!"

"And here is the blanket that Sheila and I knitted for him," said Penny, patting a neatly folded blanket at the foot of the bed of heather and bracken. "I do hope he found it nice and warm this cold winter!"

"I wonder if the little spring that gives Tammylan his drinking-water still wells up at the back of the cave," said Rory. He went to see. He flashed his torch into the darkness there, and then gave a squeal.

"What's the matter?" asked Benjy, in surprise.

"Nothing much—except that one of Tammylan's friends is here!" said Rory, with a laugh. The others came quietly to see. Tammylan had taught them to move silently when they wanted to see animals or birds.

Lying by the tiny spring that welled up from the rocky floor, was a hare. Its enormous eyes looked up patiently at the children. It could not move.

"Look—his back legs have been broken," said Sheila, sadly. "Tammylan is trying to mend then. He has put them into splints. Poor hare—he must somehow have been caught in a trap."

The children gazed down at the patient hare. It dipped its nose into the springing water and lapped a little. Benjy felt sure that it was in pain.

Penny wanted to stroke it but Benjy wouldn't let her. "No hurt animals likes to be touched," he said. "Leave it alone, Penny."

"Listen!" said Sheila, suddenly. "I can hear Tammylan I think!"

They listened—and they all knew at once that it was dear old Tammylan. No one else had that sweet clear whistle, no one else in the world could flute like a blackbird, or whistle like a blackcap! The children all rushed to the cave entrance.

"Tammylan!" they shouted. "Tammylan! We're here!"

CHAPTER V

GOOD OLD TAMMYLAN!

TAMMYLAN was coming along up the hillside, his arms full of green stuff and roots. He dropped it all when he saw the children, and a broad smile spread across his brown face. His bright eyes twinkled like the sparkles on a stream as the children flung themselves at him and hugged him.

"Well, well, well," he said, "what a storm of children breaking over me! Rory, how you've grown! Sheila, let me have a look at you! Benjy—dear old Benjy, I've thought of you so often. And my dear little Penny—not so very little now—quite grown-up!"

Chattering and laughing, the five of them sat down on a heathery bank. They were all delighted to see Tammylan again. He was a person they trusted absolutely. He would always do the right thing, never misunderstand them, always be their trusted friend. He was as natural as the animals he loved so much, as gay as the birds, as wise as the hills around. Oh, it was good to see Tammylan again!

"Tammylan, have you seen Willow Farm?" cried Penny. "Isn't it lovely?"

"It's a fine place," said Tammylan. "And a good farm too. With hard work and a bit of luck you should all do well there. The land's good. The fields are well-sheltered just where they need it, and it has always had a name for doing well with its stock. You'll all help, I suppose?"

"Of course!" said Rory. "We boys are doing lessons with the vicar again this term—and the girls are going to as well! So we shall have all our spare-time for the farm and Saturdays and Sundays as well. Aren't we lucky, Tammylan?"

"Very," said their friend. "Well, if you need any help at any time, come to me. I can work as hard as anybody, you know—and I know many strange medicines to help sick creatures."

"Oh Tammylan—we saw that poor hare in your cave," said Benjy, remembering. "Will it get better?"

"If it lives till tonight, it will mend," said Tammylan. "I have some roots here that I want to pound and mix with something else. If I can get the hare to take the mixture, it will deaden the pain and help it to live. An animal who is badly shocked, or who suffers great pain

"It's lovely to see you again, Tammylan!"

dies very easily. Poor little hare—it is a great friend of mine. You have seen him before, Benjy."

"Oh—is it the hare who came so often to your cave last year?" asked Benjy, sadly. "He was such a dear—so swift-running, and so gentle. I did love him. What happened to hurt him so badly, Tammylan?"

"I don't know," said the wild man. "It almost looks as if he had been hit hard with a stick, though I should not have thought anyone could have got near enough to him to do that. I don't know how he dragged himself here to me, poor thing. He only had his front legs to crawl with."

Penny was almost in tears. She watched the wild man pound up some roots with a heavy stone. He mixed the juice with a fine brown powder and stirred the two together. Then he went into his cave, followed by the children.

The hare gazed up at the wild man with big, pained eyes, Tammylan knelt down and took the soft head gently in his left hand. He opened the slack mouth and deftly thrust in a soft pellet of his curious mixture. He shut the hare's mouth and held it. The creature struggled weakly and then swallowed.

Tammylan let go the hare's mouth, and ran his strong brown fingers down the back of the creature's head. "You'll feel better in a little while," he said in his soft voice.

They all went out into the open air again. Benjy asked a question that had been on the tip of his tongue for some time.

"Tammylan—where's Scamper?"

"Well, well—to think I hadn't mentioned your squirrel before!" said the wild man with a laugh. "Scamper is doing exactly what his name says—scampering about the trees with all the other squirrels. He stayed with me in the cave in the cold weather, hardly stirring—but this last week it has been warm, and the little creature has often gone to play in the trees with his cousins."

"Oh," said Benjy, disappointed. "Isn't he tame any more then?"

"Of course!" said Tammylan. "You'll see him in a minute or two. I'll whistle him!"

Tammylan gave a curiously piercing whistle, loud and musical.

"It's a bit like an otter's whistle," said Benjy, remembering a night he had spent with Tammylan when he had heard otters whistling in the river to one another. "I hope Scamper hears you, Tammylan."

"He will hear me, no matter in what part of the woods he is!" said Tammylan. The wild man was right! In about half a minute Benjy gave a shout.

"Look! There comes Scamper up the hillside, look!" Sure enough they could all see the little brown squirrel bounding gracefully up the hill, his bushy tail streaming out behind him. He rushed straight up to the little group, gave a snicker of joy and leapt up to Benjy's shoulder!

"Oh you dear little thing, you've remembered me after three months!" said Benjy, joyfully. "I wondered if you would. Oh, Tammylan, isn't he lovely? He's grown—and his tail is magnificent!"

The squirrel made some funny little chattering noises, and gently bit Benjy's ear. He ran round and round the boy's neck, then up and down his back and then sat on the very top of his head! Everybody laughed.

"He is certainly delighted to see you, Benjy," said Tammylan. Scamper looked at the wild man, leapt to his shoulder and then back to Benjy again. It was almost as if he said "I'm pleased to see Benjy, but I'm very fond of you too, Tammylan!"

"Do you think he will come back to Willow Farm with me?" asked Benjy. "I do want him to."

"Oh yes," said the wild man. "But you mustn't mind if he goes off by himself at times, Benjy. He loves his own kind, you know. I will teach you the whistle I keep specially for him, and then he will always comes to you when you want him."

"I'm jolly hungry," said Penny, suddenly. "We've brought a picnic lunch, Tammylan. You'll share it with us, won't you?"

"Of course," said Tammylan. "Come with me. I know a warm and sheltered spot out of this cold March wind. It will be April next week, and then the sun will really begin to feel hot!"

He took them to a spot above his cave. Here there was a kind of hollow in the hillside, quite out of the wind, where the sun poured down. Primroses grew there by the hundred, and later on the cowslips nodded there. The children sat down on some old bracken and basked like cats in the sun.

"Lovely!" said Benjy. "Hurry up with the food, Rory."

They ate a good dinner, and talked nineteen to the dozen all the time to Tammylan, telling him about school and London, and Willow Farm. Then Tammylan in his turn told them his news.

"It's not so exciting as yours," he said, "because I have lived quietly here in my cave since you left. I was very glad of your woolly blanket, Sheila and Penny, when that cold snap came—and as for your carved stool, Rory and Benjy, I really don't know what I should have done without it! I have used it as a table, and as a stool every day!"

"Good," said the children, pleased. "Now, Tammylan, what animals have you had for company since we saw you last?"

"Well, as you know, a great many of them sleep the winter away," said Tammylan. "But the rabbits have been in to see me a great deal, and have skipped round my cave merrily. They soon disappeared when the weasel came though!"

"*Weasel!*" said Benjy, astonished. "Was a weasel tame enough to visit you?"

"Yes," said Tammylan. "I was pleased to see him too, for he was a fine little fellow. He smelt the smell of rabbits and that is how he first came into my cave. You'd have liked him, Benjy. He used to bound about like a little clown."

"Who else came to see you?" asked Penny, wishing that she had lived with Tammylan in his cave for the last three months!

"Plenty of birds," said Tammylan. "The moorhens often came. Thrushes, robins, blackbirds, chaffinches—they all hopped in at times, and for a whole month a robin slept here in the cave with me."

"Did the fox come again?" asked Rory, remembering the hunted fox to whom Tammylan had given shelter one winter's day when they had all been there.

"Yes," said Tammylan. "He comes often. He is a most beautiful creature. He always goes straight to the little water-spring at the back of the cave and laps two or three drops from it, almost as if he remembers each time how the waters helped him when he was so weary with being hunted!"

The children stayed talking in the warm hollow until almost tea-time. Then they got up and stretched their legs.

"We promised Mummy we would be back at tea-time," said Sheila. "We must go. Come and see us at Willow Farm, Tammylan, won't you? We'll be awfully busy soon, and may not have time to come and see you every day, though we'd love to. But you can come and see us whenever you like. Daddy and Mummy will love to see you—and we do want to show you everything at Willow Farm."

The children said goodbye to the wild man and left. Before they went they slipped softly into the cave to have a look at the hare. Rory shone his torch down on it.

"Oh, it looks better," he said, pleased. "Its eyes haven't got that hurt, glassy look. I believe it will mend. Poor hare—don't look so sad. One day soon you will be bounding over the fields again, as swiftly as the wind."

"I doubt that," said Tammylan. "He will never run fast again. I shall have to keep him as a pet. He will limp for the rest of his life. But he will be happy here with me if I can tame him."

The children ran home over Christmas Common, came to the top of Willow Hill and ran down it to their home. It was nice to come home to Willow Farm. The vans had gone. Bits of straw blew about in the yard. Smoke came from three chimneys now instead of one. Bill the thatcher was talking to their father in the yard. Somebody was singing in the kitchen.

"It really feels like home," said Sheila, running in at the kitchen door. She stopped when she saw somebody strange there.

A plump, red-cheeked woman smiled at her. "Come along in," she said. "I'm Harriet. I've been wanting to see you children all day!"

The children all came in. They liked the look of Harriet. A young girl of about fifteen was busy laying a tea-tray. She glanced shyly at the children.

"That's Fanny, my niece," said Harriet. "She's coming in daily to help."

"I'm Sheila, and this is my sister Penny," said Sheila. "And that's Rory, the eldest, and this is Benjy. Is that our tea being got ready?"

"It is," said Harriet. "Your mother is upstairs putting things to rights, if you want her. She was wondering if you were back."

The children ran to find their mother. They peeped into each room downstairs. Oh, how different they looked now, with all the familiar chairs and tables in them!

The children went upstairs. They looked into their bedrooms. Not only were their beds there now but their own chests and chairs and bookcases! Penny's dolls' cot stood beside her own little bed. The big ship that Rory had once made stood proudly on his mantelpiece.

"Oh, it all looks lovely!" said the children. "Mummy! Where are you?"

"Here," said Mummy, from the playroom. The children rushed in. The playroom looked fine too with all their own chairs and the two old nursery tables. The old rocking chair was there too, the two dolls' houses, the fort, and a great pile of old toy animals belonging to Penny and Benjy.

"This is going to be a lovely room for us!" said Benjy, staring out of the window down the hill to where the silver streams gleamed in the dying sun. "Mummy, how quick you've been to get everything ready like this!"

"Well, it may look as if it's ready," said his mother, with a laugh. "But it isn't really. We must put the rugs down tomorrow—and the pictures up—and you must sort out your books and put them into your bookcases, and Penny must arrange her toys in the cupboard over there. There's a lot to do yet."

"Well, we shall love doing it!" said Rory, thinking with joy of arranging all his belongings in his new bedroom. "Everything's fun at Willow Farm!"

CHAPTER VI

A SURPRISE FOR PENNY

THE next few days were great fun. The children arranged all their things to their liking. They made friends with Harriet and Fanny—though Fanny at first was too shy to say a word! Harriet was very jolly, and nearly always had some titbit ready for the children when they trooped into the kitchen.

Bill the thatcher finished the roof, and did not find anything exciting in the thatch at all, much to Penny's disappointment.

"I'm glad that job's finished," he said. "Now I can get on to the farm-work. There's a lot of sowing to be done—and I must get the garden ready for your mother. She wants to grow all kinds of things there!"

"Isn't there anything *we* can do?" asked Rory. "I want to WORK! I wish we could get in our hens and ducks and pigs and cows and things—then we could help to look after them."

The children asked their parents when the birds and animals of the farm were coming.

"Soon," said their father. "Your uncle Tim is bringing over the poultry tomorrow. The hen-houses are ready now. Which of you is going to take care of the hens?"

"I will." said Sheila at once. "I like hens—though I like ducks better. Let me take care of the hens, Daddy."

"Well, Sheila, if you do, you must really learn about them properly," said her father. "It was all very well at Cherry Tree Farm for you and others to throw corn to the hens when you felt like it, and go and find nice warm eggs to carry in to your Aunt Bess—but if you are really and truly going to see the hens and make them your special care, you will have to know quite a lot."

"I see, Daddy," said Sheila. "Well—have you got a book about them?"

"I've two or three," said Daddy. "I'll get them for you."

"Sheila, could I help with the hens too?" asked Penny. "I want to do something. The boys say they are going to do the pigs and milk the cows when they come."

Sheila badly wanted to manage the hens entirely by herself, but when she saw Penny's small, earnest face her heart melted.

"Well," she said, "yes, you can. You can read the books too."

Penny was overjoyed. She felt tremendously important. She was going to read books about poultry-keeping! She longed to tell somebody that. She would tell Tammylan as soon as ever she saw him.

Daddy fetched them the books. They looked very grown-up and rather dull. But Sheila and Penny didn't mind. Now they would know all about hens! Sheila handed Penny the one that looked the easier. It had pictures of hens inside.

"Daddy, you'll let us see to the pigs when they come, won't you?" asked Benjy. "And milk the cows too. We can clean out the sheds quite well. I did it once or twice at Cherry Tree Farm."

"You can try," said Daddy. "Soon the farm will be working properly—cows in the fields, pigs in the sty, horses in the stable, hens and ducks running about, butter being made, sheep being dipped—my word, what a busy life we shall lead! And we shall all have breakfast at seven o'clock in the morning!"

"Goodness!" said Sheila, who was a lie-abed. "That means getting up at half-past six!"

"Yes—and going to bed early too," said her father. "Farmers have to be up and about soon after dawn—and they can't be up early if they go to bed late!"

None of the children liked the idea of going to bed early. But still, if they were going to be farmers, they must do as farmers did!

Sheila and Penny went up to the playroom with the hen books. Penny struggled hard with the reading. She could read very well indeed—but oh dear, what long words there were—and what a lot of chapters about things called incubators and brooders. She soon gave it up.

"Sheila," she said, in a small voice. "I really can't understand this book. Is yours any easier?"

Sheila was finding her book dreadfully difficult too. It seemed to be written for people who had kept hens for years, not for anybody just beginning. She felt that she wouldn't know how to feed them properly—she wouldn't know when a hen wanted to sit on eggs, she wouldn't know how to tell if they were ill.

But she wasn't going to tell that to Penny! So she looked up and smiled. "Oh Penny dear," she said, "what a baby you are! *I'll* read the books, if you can't, and I'll tell you what they say. I can tell you in words that you'll understand."

Penny went red. "All right," she said. "You will just have to tell me."

The little girl was quite ashamed because she couldn't understand the books. She left the playroom and went downstairs. She thought she would go and talk to the old shepherd up on the hill. So off she went.

The sheep were peacefully grazing on the hillside. Little lambs skipped about, and Penny laughed to see them. She wished and wished that she could have one of her own. She had fed some at Cherry Tree Farm from a baby's bottle, and how she had loved that!

"Really, I think lambs are much nicer than hens," said Penny to herself. "I know Sheila likes hens—but I do think they are a bit dull. They all see exactly alike, somehow. Now, lambs are like people—all different."

She stood and watched the lambs skipping about. Then she looked at the sheep.

"It's a great pity that lambs grow into sheep," she thought. "Sheep are like hens—all exactly the same. I suppose the shepherd can tell one from the other—but I certainly couldn't!"

She looked to see where the shepherd was. He was at the top of the hill, where a rough fold had been made of wattle hurdles. Penny ran to it.

"Hallo," she said, when she came to the shepherd. "I've come to see you."

"Well, little Missy," said the shepherd, leaning on his

staff and looking at the little girl with eyes as grey as his hair. "And what's your name?"

"Penny," said Penny. "What's yours?"

"Davey," said the shepherd. "That's a funny name you've got. When you were small, I suppose they called you Farthing? And then when you grew did they call you Ha'penny? Now you're Penny. When will you be Tuppence?"

Penny laughed. She liked Davey. "No, I didn't have all those names," she said. "My real name is Penelope, but I'm called Penny for short."

"Well, I shall call you Tuppenny," said the shepherd. "A penny is too cheap!"

They both laughed. A big collie-dog came running up to them and licked Penny's hand. She patted him.

"That's my best dog, Rascal," said Davey. "He's a wonder with the sheep!"

"Is he really? What does he do to them, then?" asked Penny.

"Oh, you come along one day when I'm moving the sheep from one hill to another," said Davey. "Then you'll see what old Rascal does. Do you know, if I were ill and wanted my sheep taken from here to the top of the next hill, I've only got to tell Rascal—and before two hours had gone by, those sheep would all be safely down this hill and up the next!"

"Goodness!" said Penny. "I'd love to see him do that. Davey, there's another dog over there. What's his name?"

"That's Nancy," said Davey. "She's good too, but not so obedient as Rascal. And look, over there is Tinker. He's not a sheep-dog, but he's almost as good as the others."

"Rascal, Nancy and Tinker," said Penny, thinking what nice names they were. "Davey, is it easy to keep sheep?"

"Yes, if you know how," said Davey. "I've been doing it all my life, little Tuppeny, and I've made all the mistakes there are to be made—but there's not much I don't know about sheep now!"

"Do you know, I used to feed lambs out of a bottle at Cherry Tree Farm?" said Penny. "I did love it. I do wish I was like the Mary in the nursery rhyme who had a lamb of her own. I do so love lambs."

"Well, you come and have a look at this poor little lambie," said Davey, taking Penny's hand. "Now, if you'd been here six weeks ago I'd have asked you to take it and care for it, for in the lambing season I've no time for sickly lambs. Still, I've tried to do my best for this one."

He took Penny to a small fold in which lay one lamb. It was some weeks old, but was tiny, and very weakly.

"Its mother had three lambs," said the shepherd. "She liked two of them but she just wouldn't have anything to do with this one. So I took it away and gave it to another ewe whose lamb had died. But I had to skin the dead lamb first and cover this one with the hide."

"But what a funny thing to do!" cried Penny. "Why did you do that?"

"Because the mother would only take a lamb that smelt like hers," said Davey. "Well, she sniffed at this one, covered with the skin of her dead lamb, and she took to it and mothered it."

"Oh, I'm glad," said Penny.

"Ah, but wait a bit," said Davey. "She mothered it for a week. Then she took a dislike to it and butted it away with her head every time it came near, poor thing. It was half-starved, and I had to bring it away and try to feed it by hand out of a bottle."

"Did it wear the skin of the dead lamb all the two weeks?" asked Penny.

"Oh no—as soon as the mother sheep took the lamb, I stripped off the skin," said Davey. "But there must be something about this wee thing that the ewes dislike. No one will feed it."

"Davey, I suppose I couldn't possibly have it for my

own, could I?" asked Penny, her eyes sparkling. "I could get a baby's milk-bottle—and Harriet would let me have milk. Oh, do let me!"

"Well, I'll speak to your father," said the shepherd. "It would help me if you took it and cared for it. I've not much time now—and the lamb will die if it doesn't begin to grow a bit soon!"

Penny looked at the long-legged lamb in the fold. It had a little black face, a long wriggly tail, a thin little body, and legs just like her toy lamb at home.

"It's not a very pretty lamb," she said. "It looks sort of miserable. Lambs are always so full of spring and leap and frisk, aren't they—but this one isn't."

"That's because it isn't well," said Davey. "I'll talk to your father about it, Tuppenny. Ah—there he is. I'll have a word with him now. See—is that somebody calling you down there?"

It was Penny's mother. Penny rushed down the hill to see what she wanted. "Mummy, Mummy!" she yelled, as soon as she got near, "Davey the shepherd says perhaps I may have a lamb of my own to feed. Oh Mummy, do you suppose I can? Davey is going to talk to Daddy about it. He says the lamb will die if somebody doesn't take care of it properly."

Sheila overheard what Penny said. "I thought you were going to help with the hens," she said.

"So I will," said Penny. "But I do feel I shall understand one lamb better than a whole lot of hens, Sheila. Anyway, it won't take long to feed each day."

Penny's mother had called her in to make her bed. She had forgotten to do it. It was the rule that each of the children should make their own beds and tidy their own rooms. Penny made her bed quickly and dusted and tidied her room. She looked out of the window to see if Daddy and the shepherd were still talking. No—Daddy had left Davey and was now walking down to the farm.

Penny put her head out of the window. "Daddy!" she yelled. "Can I have the lamb?"

"Yes, if you'll really care for it properly," said her father. The little girl gave an enormous yell and rushed downstairs, nearly knocking over poor Fanny as she went. "I'm going to have a lamb!" she yelled to Fanny."

She tore up the hill as if a hundred dogs were after her. She meant to get that lamb before anybody changed their minds about it!

"What a whirlwind!" said Davey, as Penny raced up to him. "Well, you're to have the lamb. Mind you bring it up to me sometimes so that I can see how well it is growing."

"Oh, I will, I will," said Penny. "I'm going to buy it a feeding-bottle out of my own money."

"You needn't do that," said Davey. "You can have this one." He held out a feeding-bottle to Penny. It had a big teat through which the lamb could suck the milk just as a baby sucks from a bottle. "I've fed him this morning. Give him another bottle of milk at dinner-time, and another at tea-time. Just give him as much as Harriet can spare."

Penny took the bottle. Then Davey undid one of the hurdles of the fold and took up the lamb. He tied a rope loosely round its neck.

"He won't follow you till he knows you," he said. "Take him gently down to the farm. Ask your mother if you can keep him in the little orchard till he knows you. Then he'll keep by you and not wander, as you go about the farmyard."

Penny was most excited and joyful. She had always wanted a lamb of her very one. She wondered what she would call the little creature.

"I'll call it Skippetty," she said. "It isn't very skippetty now—but perhaps it soon will be."

She took hold of the rope and tried to lead the lamb down the hill. At first it held back and tugged at the rope as if it wanted a tug-of-war with Penny. But soon it followed her peacefully enough and once it even ran in front of her.

When she got down to the farm, the other three children came to stare in astonishment.

"What are you doing with that lamb?" asked Benjy. "What a dear little black-faced creature!"

"It's mine," said Penny, proudly. "Its name is Skippetty."

"Yours!" said Rory in amazement. "Who gave it to you!"

"Davey the shepherd," said Penny. "He's awfully nice. He's got three dogs, Rascal, Nancy and Tinker—and he says when he moves the sheep, we are to go and watch how well his dogs work for him. He gave me this lamb for my own to look after because it is such a poor little thing and he hasn't got time for it."

"You *are* lucky!" said Benjy. "I like it almost as much as I like Scamper."

Scamper was on his shoulder. The squirrel had not left Benjy once since he had brought it back to the farm. It even slept with Benjy at night!"

"I'm going to show Skippetty to Mummy," said Penny, and off she went. She took the lamb into the lounge and Mummy cried out in surprise.

"Oh no, Penny dear—you really can't bring the lamb into the house! Keep it in the orchard."

Well, it was all very well for Mummy to say that Penny wasn't to bring Skippetty into the house! The lamb lived in the orchard for a day or two and then Penny set it free to see if it would follow her, like Mary's little lamb. And it did!

It followed her everywhere! It followed her to the barn. It followed her into the kitchen. It even went up the stairs after her to the playroom! It just wouldn't be left without Penny.

The little girl loved it. She fed it as often as Harriet would spare the milk. It was such fun, Harriet emptied the milk into the bottle and then Penny would take it to the lamb. It ran to her at once, and sometimes even put its funny long legs up on to her waist to get at the milk more quickly. It emptied the bottle in a trice, sucking noisily at the teat.

It grew even in three days! It became frisky and skippetty, and Penny loved it.

The others sang the nursery rhyme whenever they saw Penny coming with her lamb trotting behind her.

"Penny had a little lamb,
Its fleece was white as snow,
And everywhere that Penny went,
The lamb was sure to go!"

Mother grew used to the lamb trotting in and out of the house—but she scolded Penny for letting it go into the bathroom when Penny bathed at night.

"Oh, Penny darling, I really can't have that!" she cried. "You'll be bathing it in the bath next!"

Penny went red. She had secretly thought that it *would* be great fun to bath the lamb, especially one evening when it had rolled in some mud and got dirty.

"All right, I won't take it into the bathroom again," she said.

Harriet joined in the conversation. "*Nor* in the larder, *nor* in the dairy, *nor* in the broom-cupboard!" she said, her eyes twinkling.

"I'll make my lamb be good," promised Penny, laughing. "I'll make it just as good as I am!"

"Good gracious!" said Harriet, smiling, "what a monkey of a lamb it will be!"

CHAPTER VII

SHEILA FINDS A FRIEND

PENNY'S lamb had been a great excitement—and something else was too! The hens came. This may not sound a very exciting thing, but to the four children at Willow Farm, it was very thrilling. Hens of their own! Hens that would lay eggs and make money—this was a real bit of farm-life to the children.

Sheila had studied the three books and had learnt very little from them. She hadn't liked to own up that the books were too difficult—but she had found help most unexpectedly.

It came from Fanny, the girl who came in daily to help Harriet. She had come in to clean the playroom when Sheila had been sitting there trying to puzzle out what the poultry books meant.

"Oh Fanny!" sighed Sheila. "I wish I knew a lot more about hens. I'm going to look after them, you know, and I really must learn about them, or they won't lay eggs, and won't do well at all. And I do want to help my mother and father to make our farm pay."

"Well, Miss Sheila, what do you want to know?" asked Fanny, shyly. "My mother keeps hens, and I've looked after them since I was a tiny thing. You don't need to worry about your hens, surely—you've got a fine hen-house—and plenty of coops—and Harriet will cook the scraps for you—and there's corn in the bins."

"Fanny, tell me about hens," begged Sheila. "From the very beginning. I don't want to make any mistakes."

Fanny laughed. "Oh, you learn by making mistakes,"

she said. "First of all, what hens are you going to have? There are a good many kinds you know. Are you going to keep yours for egg-laying or for meat—you know, eating?"

"Oh, egg-laying," said Sheila. "I want lots and lots of eggs. Uncle Tim is bringing the hens over tomorrow. They are to be Buff Orpingtons."

"Oh, those nice fat brown, comfortable-looking hens!" said Fanny, pleased. "They are like ours. They lay a fine lot of eggs. You know Miss Sheila, they're the best hens to have in the winter-time anyway, because they'll lay when other kinds won't."

"Well, that's good," said Sheila. "But will they sit on eggs well too?"

"Oh yes," said Fanny. "Ours do, anyway. Oh Miss Sheila, it will be fun to set some eggs, won't it, and see the chicks come out?"

"Goodness, yes," said Sheila. "Fancy, Fanny, I don't even know how many eggs to put under a sitting hen!"

"Oh, I can tell you things like that," said Fanny. "You put thirteen good fresh eggs. And you'll have to see the hen doesn't leave her eggs for more than twenty minutes!"

"Why, would they get cold?" asked Sheila.

"Freezing cold," said Fanny. "Then they wouldn't hatch out. That's why we put a sitting hen into a coop, Miss. So that she can't get out and leave her eggs."

"But how does she get food and water?" asked Sheila.

Fanny laughed. "That's easy enough!" she said. "You just let her out for a feed of corn and a drink and a stretch of her legs each day."

"What would happen if I forgot to do that?" asked Sheila.

"Well, the poor thing would sit till she got so hungry she'd peck her own eggs and eat them," said Fanny. "It's just common sense, Miss, that's all. Did you know that a hen turns her eggs over now and then, to warm them evenly? I've often watched our sitting hens do that. You wouldn't think they were clever enough to do that, would you?"

"How long does the hen sit on her eggs?" asked Sheila. "Ages and ages, I suppose."

"Oh no—only for three weeks," said Fanny. "Oh, Miss Sheila, it's fun when the eggs hatch and the baby chicks come out! You'll love that."

"Yes, I shall," said Sheila, thinking with delight of dozens of tiny cheeping chicks running about the farm-yard. "Oh Fanny, I've learnt more about hens from you in five minutes than I've learnt from all these difficult books!"

"If I've got time, I'll come and see the hen-house with you this afternoon," said Fanny. "You'll want some peat-moss for the floor, you know. That's the best stuff to have—you only need to change it once or twice a year."

"Oh Fanny, hurry up with your work then, and we'll go and plan for the hens!" said Sheila. "I'll tell Daddy we want some peat-moss."

Fanny was just as pleased as Sheila to make plans for the hens. She had been used to keeping them all her life, but only in a tiny back-yard with a very small hen-house. Now they would be kept properly, with plenty of room for coops and chicks too. What fun! She flew over her work that morning and her Aunt Harriet was very pleased with her.

"You've earned your time off this afternoon, Fanny," she said. "You've been a good girl this morning. You scrubbed my kitchen floor well for me, and that stove shines like glass!"

"I'm going to help Miss Sheila get ready for her hens," said Fanny. "Goodness, Aunt Harriet, you wait and see what a lot of eggs and chicks we get!"

"Don't you count your chickens before they are hatched!" said Harriet.

Sheila and Fanny and Penny spent a very happy afternoon indeed. The three of them cleaned out the hen-house. It was not very dirty, and had already been white-washed inside. Fanny got some peat-moss from the village in a small sack and brought it back to the farm. It was lovely stuff, dark brown and velvety. The three girls let it run through their fingers joyfully.

"I should love to tread on this and scratch about in it if I was a hen," said Penny. "Do we scatter it over the floor?"

"Yes, like this," said Fanny. Soon the hen-house floor was strewn with the dark brown peat-moss and looked very nice indeed.

"Do we put it into the nesting-boxes as well?" asked Penny, looking into the row of neat, empty nesting-boxes.

"No. We'll get some straw for those," said Fanny, happily. She was enjoying herself. She was a real country-girl, liking anything to do with farm-life. The three girls found some straw in a shed and took enough back for the nesting-boxes. They patted it down flat, and tried to make it comfortable for the hens.

"I wish I was small enough to get right into one of the nesting-boxes, and sit down on the straw to see how it felt," said Penny.

The others laughed. "You're funny, Penny," said Sheila. "You hate to be treated as if you were little—and yet you are always wanting to be smaller than you are—a toy in a cupboard, or a hen in a nesting-box!"

The hen-house had a hen-run, with wire netting around. It was overgrown with grass.

"That won't matter," said Fanny. "The hens will soon peck that up! Anyway, you'll let them free to wander over the yard, won't you, Miss Sheila?"

"Oh yes," said Sheila. "But I hope they won't lay their eggs away anywhere—you know, under a hedge or something. It would be a pity."

"Well, we'll just have to watch out for that," said Fanny. "Now, what about food? Look—there is corn in this big bin. We'll give them some of that each day! Corn helps them to lay often, and we shall get bigger eggs if we give them plenty."

"What else do we give them?" asked Penny.

"Well, my Aunt Harriet will cook up all the household scraps," said Fanny. "You know—potato peel, milk-pudding scrapings, crusts of bread—anything we have over. It will all go into the hen-food. Then we will mix it with mash—and give them a good helping early in the morning, and after tea. We'll let them have the corn at midday. They'll like that."

"It does sound exciting," said Penny. "What about water? They want plenty of that, don't they?"

"Yes—a big dishful," said Fanny. "Look—that trough will do. We'll fill it full each day. They must have fresh water. And I'll get my aunt to give us all the cabbage stalks and things like that. The hens will love to peck them."

"We'll clean the house each day," said Sheila. "I'll scrape the dropping-board with this little hoe. Oh, I *do* hope my hens do well!"

"They should do," said Fanny. "The thing is not to make too much fuss of them; but to be sure to give them a clean house, good food, fresh water and plenty of place to run. Well, they'll have all that. Oh—I've quite forgotten something important!"

"What?" asked the two girls.

"We must give them grit to help them to digest their food—and lime or oyster-shell broken up as well," said Fanny.

"Broken oyster-shell! Whatever for?" said Penny in surprise. "Hens won't like sea-shell, will they?"

Fanny laughed. "They don't like it as food," she said, "but they need it to help them to make the shells for their eggs. If they don't get it the eggs will be soft-shelled and no use."

"I saw some stuff in a bag where we saw the corn," said Sheila. "I think it must have been broken oyster-shell

—and there was some grit there too. Let's get it. We can put it into this wooden box inside the house—then the rain won't spoil it."

By tea-time there was nothing else to be done to prepare for the hens. The boys came in and the girls showed them everything. Scamper leapt down from Benjy's shoulder to examine the hen-house. He went into one of the nesting-boxes and peeped out of it cheekily.

"Are you going to lay a squirrel-egg, Scamper?" laughed Benjy. "Funny little thing, aren't you?"

"Uncle Tim is bringing the hens tomorrow afternoon," said Sheila. "Oh Rory—won't it be fun if we have some baby chicks? I should so love that."

"Well, maybe one or two of your hens will go broody and want to sit all day long," said Benjy. "Then you can give her some eggs, and she'll hatch them out for you."

"We can get out the coops then," said Sheila. "You know, Benjy, Fanny's been awfully helpful. I couldn't understand a thing in those books—but she's told me everything."

"Good." said Benjy. "Hie, Penny, where are you going? It's tea-time."

Penny was tearing off to the little orchard. She climbed over the gate. "I'm going to fetch Skippetty!" she shouted. "It's his tea-time too. Fanny, ask Harriet if she can let me have another bottle of milk for him. He looks so hungry, poor lamb!"

The lamb came tearing up to Penny. She took it to the farmyard. Benjy was there with Scamper. Scamper leapt from his shoulder and sat on the lamb's back. "He wants a ride!" laughed Penny. "Oh, how I wish I could take a picture of them both!"

"Aren't you two ever coming?" called Sheila. "There are hot scones and honey for tea—and I can tell you there won't be any left if you don't come AT ONCE!"

CHAPTER VIII

THE COMING OF THE HENS

NEXT day the hens came. Uncle Tim brought them over in a great big box. Aunt Bess was with him. It was the first time they had visited Willow Farm since the family had settled in. They jumped down from the wagon they had come in, and everyone ran to greet them.

"Uncle Tim! Aunt Bess! Look at my own pet lamb!" yelled Penny.

"Uncle Tim—I've got Scamper again!" cried Benjy.

"Hallo, Tim, hallo, Bess!" cried the children's parents. "Welcome to Willow Farm! We are getting straight at last! Come along in and have something to eat and drink."

Everyone went indoors, talking and laughing. After a while Sheila and Penny slipped out. They went to the kitchen. Harriet was there, cleaning the silver and Fanny was helping her.

"Harriet! Could you spare Fanny just a few minutes?" begged Sheila. "The hens have come! I thought it would be such fun to put them into the hen-house ourselves! I do want to see how they like it."

Harriet laughed. "Yes—Fanny can come. Go along, Fanny—but see you finish that silver when you come back!"

"Oh yes, aunt!" said Fanny. She ran out into the drive with the two children. The hens were still in the big box, strapped on to the back of the wagon.

They were clucking loudly. "Oh, there's a fine cock too!" cried Sheila, pleased. "See his beautiful tail-feathers

The fine cock strutted proudly around his new home

sticking out of the crack in the crate! Fanny, how are we to get the hens to the house?"

"We'll carry them," said Fanny. "I'll show you how."

The three of them undid the rope round the crate, and Fanny forced up the top. She put in her arm and got a hen. It squawked loudly and struggled wildly.

But Fanny knew how to calm it and carry it. She showed the others how to take the hens by the top part of their legs, very firmly, and hold down the wings at the same time. "Put the bird under your left arm, so," she said. "That's right. Now you've got your other hand to hold the legs. We'll take them one at a time."

The three enjoyed carrying the squawking hens. It was fun. One by one they were all taken to the big hen-house. There were twenty Buff Orpingtons, and one fine cock.

"Aren't they lovely hens?" said Sheila joyfully. "They look so brown and shiny, so fat and comfortable. I do like them. Look how straight up their combs are."

"They are nice young hens," said Fanny, pleased. "They should lay well. Twenty is just about the right number for the house and yard. If you have too many and they are overcrowded, they don't keep healthy. My word, your uncle has picked you out some beauties—they look as healthy as can be. It's always best to start with the finest hens you can possibly get."

The hens clucked about the house. Then they found the opening that led down the ladder-plank to the run. Down it they went, stepping carefully, their heads bobbing as they walked. "Cluck-cluck!" they said as they each entered the run. "Cluck-luck, what-luck!"

"Did you hear that!" said Penny. "They think they are lucky to come here!"

"Cluck-luck, what-luck!" said the hens again, and they pecked at some cabbage stalks that Fanny had brought from the kitchen.

"We'll give them some corn to scratch for," said Fanny. The three went to the corn-bin and each got a handful.

They scattered the corn in the run. The hens rans to it, clucking and scratching eagerly.

Sheila counted them. "One cock—and only nineteen hens," she said. "Where's the other?"

It was in one of the nesting-boxes, laying an egg. Penny gave a shout of delight.

"It *must* feel at home to do that already! Sheila—let's see if they laid any in the crate on the way over."

The girls went to look—and sure enough there were two nice big brown eggs on the floor of the crate! How pleased they were!

"I'm going to keep a proper egg-book," said Sheila. "I shall put down in it every egg that is laid! Then I shall be able to find out how much money my hens make for me, because I shall know the market-price of eggs each week, and reckon it up. Oh—it will be fun! I like doing something *real* like this!"

Just then everyone else came out from the farmhouse. Uncle Tim had said that he really must take the hens out of their crate—and lo and behold the crate was empty!

"Oh! The girls have done it all themselves, the mean things!" cried Rory, with a laugh. "No wonder they slipped out so quietly! Oh, look at all the hens in the run, Uncle. Don't they look fine?"

Everyone went to look at the brown hens. They seemed quite at home already, pecking about for the corn.

"One of them is laying an egg," said Sheila proudly. "I shall enter it in my egg-book."

"Sheila is going to manage the hens for us," said her father. "We shall just see how well she can do it!"

"Does she understand everything she has to do?" said Aunt Bess. "You know, the children only just gave the hens corn at times, and took the eggs in, when they were with us—they didn't really know much about the keeping of them."

"Have you got grit and oyster-shell, Sheila?" asked

Uncle Tim. "Fresh water? Corn? Mash? Ah—I see you have studied some books!"

"Well," said Sheila, "I did try to study the books Daddy gave me—but actually Fanny told me most of what I had to do. Uncle Tim, I shall make my hens do even better than yours. You just see!"

"I hope you do," said her uncle. "Then I will come and take a few lessons from you on poultry-farming, Sheila!"

It really was fun having hens to look after. Sheila said that she knew which was which after a few days, though the others could never tell more than one or two from the rest, and they secretly thought that Sheila couldn't either.

It was lovely to go and look in the nesting-boxes for the eggs. One day Sheila actually got twenty eggs! She was so delighted that she could hardly write it down in her egg-book! She and Penny used to go to the nesting-boxes morning and evening and take the eggs in. If they were to be sold, the children wiped them clean and sorted them into sizes.

"I do like eating the eggs that my own hens lay," said Sheila, each morning. "And I must say that the brown eggs always *seem* to taste nicer, though I can't think why they should."

The hens were soon let loose in the farmyard. Then they were very happy indeed. They scratched about everywhere, and the place was full of their contented clucking. The cock was a fine fellow. He stretched his neck and crowed loudly, and his tail-feathers were really magnificent. They were purple and green and blue.

"He's a real gentleman, you know, Penny," said Sheila. "He never helps himself first to anything but always waits till his hens have eaten. And look—when he finds a grain of corn, he doesn't eat it himself. Watch—he's found one—and he's calling to his favourite hen to come and have it. Really, he has most beautiful manners!"

The two girls found that they were quite busy with the hens. The house was cleaned of droppings each day.

Fresh water was put into the trough in the run, and into the dish in the house too. The box was kept full of oyster-shell. Harriet cooked the scraps, and gave them to Sheila before breakfast. Then the two girls mixed the smelly stuff with the mash out of the bin and gave a good share to the hungry hens. In the middle of the day they gave them corn, and a helping of mash again in the evening.

At night either Sheila or Penny shut the hens into their house. They liked seeing the big brown birds perching so solemnly there. They always counted them to make quite sure that every hen was in for the night.

Their parents were pleased with the way they looked after the poultry. "We'll have ducks later on!" they said. "Perhaps you will be able to manage those as well!"

The boys were anxious to do their share too. They were glad to hear that the cows were coming at once, and that their father had bought a sow and ten little piglets.

"The farm will really be a farm then!" said Rory. "How are the cows coming, Daddy? By train?"

"No—they are walking," said his father. "It is not far from the market where I have bought them, and they are coming along by the roads and the lanes."

The children liked to think of their cows walking to find Willow Farm. "How pleased they will be when they arrive here and see their new home!" said Penny. "I'm sure they will feel just as excited as we did!"

The cows were to be short-horns. Uncle Tim said that they were excellent milkers, and made good beef.

"What colour will they be?" asked Rory.

"Oh, mostly red and white, I expect," said his mother. "I must say it will be nice to look from the window and see cows standing in the pasture. I always like cows standing about the countryside!"

"I'm looking forward to milking them," said Benjy. "It's quite easy!"

"I suppose they will feed on the grass?" asked Penny. "They won't cost much!"

"Oh, the grass won't be good enough yet for them to feed on that alone," said her father. "We must give them swedes or mangold-wurzels. The boys can cart them each day to the fields and throw them out on the grass."

"Oooh," said Benjy. "That will be fun!"

The cow-sheds were all clean, and prepared for the cows. They were to be milked there. The pails were scoured and shining, everything was ready.

"Once we have the cows to give us milk we shall be able to have our own milk, take our own cream, and make our own butter!" said Mother. "I am looking forward to that."

"When will the cows come?" asked Benjy. "I want to watch for them."

"Sometime tomorrow afternoon, I expect," said his father. "It's a good thing we have so many streams on our farm. We shan't have to cart water to the field-troughs—the cows can water themselves at the stream."

"I wish tomorrow would come!" sighed Penny. "I want to see our cows. Do you think they'll have names already, Rory? Or can we give them names? I'd like to name them all. I know such pretty cow-names."

"What names do you know?' said Rory smiling at Penny's earnest face.

"Oh, Daisy and Buttercup and Pimpernel and Kitty and Bluebell," began Penny.

"Why, those are the names of the cows at Cherry Tree Farm!" said Rory. "I'd think of a few new ones if I were you."

So Penny thought of some more. "Honeysuckle, Rhododendron, Columbine, Snapdragon," she began, but the others squealed with laughter.

"Fancy standing at the field-gate and shouting 'Rhododendron, Rhododendron!' " said Sheila. "Everybody would think you had gone mad."

"Well, anyway. I shall name *some* of the cows," said

Penny, firmly. "I do so want to do that. I shall wait for them tomorrow, and see which looks like one of my names!"

CHAPTER IX

SIXTEEN COWS FOR WILLOW FARM

THE cows arrived the next day, just before tea. Rory saw them first. He was swinging on the gate, waiting to welcome the cows to their new home. The others had gone to watch Skippetty frisking among the hens in the farmyard. The lamb was now much bigger, and was as springy and as frisky as any other lamb on the farm.

Everyone loved him, for he was a friendly and affectionate creature. He had even gone into Penny's father's study one morning and pushed his little black face into the farmer's elbow!

"Hie! The cows are coming, the cows are coming!" yelled Rory, almost falling off the gate in his excitement. "Hurry up, you others—the cows are coming. They're MARVELLOUS!"

Sheila, Benjy and Rory tore to the gate. They saw the cows rounding the corner of the lane. They came slowly, swaying a little from side to side as they walked.

"They're red, and red-and-white!" shouted Rory. "Just the kind I like. Oh, aren't they nice and fat?"

They certainly looked good cows. They gazed at the children as they went through the field-gate, and whisked their tails. They smelt nice.

They were glad to get into the field and pull at the grass. "They twist their tongues round the grass when they pick it!" said Penny. "Oh look—there's Tammylan at the back with the herdsman!"

Sure enough it was old Tammylan, come to see how the farm was getting on! He smiled at the children.

"So you've got your cows now!" he said. "And your hens too. And does this lamb belong to *you*, Penny? It seems to follow you close!"

"Yes, Skippetty is mine," said Penny, giving Tammylan a hug and then a hug to the lamb. "Tammylan, aren't our cows beautiful?"

"Yes—they look fine creatures," said Tammylan. "Have you plenty of names for them, Penny?"

"Oh, don't ask her that!" said Rory. "She keeps on and on thinking of names! I say, Tammylan, won't it be fun to milk the cows each day?"

"Rather!" said Tammylan. "Look at them all—how pleased they are to be able to stand and graze, after their long walk. They will soon get all their four stomachs into working order now!"

"*Four* stomachs! Whatever do you mean, Tammylan?" asked Sheila, astonished. "Has a cow got *four* stomachs!"

"Well—perhaps it would be truer to say that she has four compartments in her stomach!" said Tammylan, with a laugh. "Watch a cow eating, Sheila. She only bites the grass now and swallows it—she doesn't chew it. Watch one and see."

The children watched the cows. They saw that each one curled her tongue around the blades of grass, pulled them into her mouth, and then swallowed straightaway.

"And yet I've seen a cow chewing and chewing and chewing!" said Benjy. "It's called chewing the cud, isn't it, Tammylan?"

"Yes," said Tammylan. "What happens is that when she swallows the grass straightaway it goes down into the first part of her stomach. Then, when she is in her byre, or lying down resting, the swallowed grass comes up again into her mouth in balls all ready for chewing. Then she has a fine time chewing for a while. She enjoys that. You wait and see how she loves it, chewing with half-shut

C

eyes, thinking of the golden sunshine and the fields she loves!"

"Does it go back to the first part of her stomach again?" asked Penny, wishing that she had four stomachs too. "I'd love to swallow a sweet and then have it back to chew whenever I felt like it."

Tammylan laughed. "I expect you would!" he said. "No—when the cow has finished chewing the cud, the food goes down to the next part of her stomach, and then on to the third and the fourth. Have you ever seen a cow's upper teeth, Penny?"

"No—what are they like?" asked Penny, surprised. The wild man went to a cow and took its nose gently into his hand. He opened her mouth and pushed back the upper lip. "Tell me what her upper teeth are like!" he said, with a smile.

"Gracious! The cow hasn't any!" said Sheila.

"No—just a sort of bare pad of flesh," said Rory.

"How funny!" said Penny. "But a horse has upper teeth. I know, because I once saw a horse put back its lips and it had big teeth at the bottom and at the top too."

"Yes, a horse is different," said Tammylan. "It only has one stomach. And its hooves are different too. Look at this cow's hoof!"

He lifted up the front foot of the surprised cow. The children saw that it was split in two.

"Why is that?" asked Rory, astonished. "A horse only has one round bit of hoof—the cow's is split in two."

"She so often walks on soft, wet ground," said Tammylan. "Her split hoof helps her to do that without sticking to it."

"I like the way cows whisk their tails about," said Penny. "This one whisked hers round so far that it hit me. I do wish I had a tail like a cow."

"So that you could go round whisking people, I suppose?" said Tammylan. "Now Penny, I will set you a little problem. I would like to know if a cow and a horse get up from the ground in the same way. Will you please watch and tell me next time you see me?"

"I should have thought they would both have got up exactly the same way!" said the little girl, surprised.

"Well, they don't," said Tammylan. "You just see!"

"We've got sixteen cows," said Rory, who had been counting. "They are all fat and red and nice. I do think they look funny from behind—sort of wooden."

"Let's go and ask the herdsman when they have to be milked," said Sheila. "I'm just longing to do that!"

The herdsman was talking to their father. He was a tiny little fellow, with broad shoulders and long arms. Although he was small he was tremendously strong. The children's father was keeping him on the farm, for he was a useful man with cows, and good at many other jobs too. His name was Jim.

"Can we help to milk the cows?" cried Benjy. "When is it time?"

"Oh, not till well after tea," said the man, smiling. "Are you sure you know how to? Milking isn't as easy as it looks, you know!"

"Of *course* I know how to!" said Benjy, scornfully. "And I get a jolly good froth on top of my pail too!"

"Ah, that's fine," said Jim. "A good milker always gets a froth. Well—you shall help if you like. I can do with one or two good milkers! Are you going to be up at five o'clock in the morning to help me, young sir?"

That made Benjy look a little blue. Five o'clock in the morning!

"Well—if I do, shall I have to go to bed very very early?" he asked his mother.

"I'm afraid so, Benjy," she said. "An hour earlier."

"Oh. Then I'm very sorry, Jim, but I think I'll only help you in the evenings," said Benjy, who simply couldn't bear the idea of going to bed an hour sooner than the others.

"That's all right," said Jim. "I can get someone else, I daresay, to give me a hand in the morning!"

The children were all pleased when milking-time came. They took the cows down to the cow-sheds, and got the shining pails and the little milking stools.

Penny hadn't milked before. All the others had. Benjy was a fine milker. His hands were strong, yet gentle. Sheila was quite a good milker too, but Rory was poor. He could *not* make a froth come on the top of the milk in his pail as the others could. It was most annoying!

"I only get plain milk!" he said, "and I don't get my pail full nearly as quickly as you others! Look at Jim—he has milked three cows already and I haven't even done one!"

"You've got rather an awkward cow," said Jim. "She doesn't like to give her milk to a stranger. I'll finish her for you. The last milk from a cow is always the richest, you know, so we must be sure to get it. Try the next cow—Daisy, she's called. She's an easy one to milk."

"I love this warm milk," said Penny, putting her hand against the warm sides of a pailful of milk. "Jim, can I try to milk an easy cow?"

"You come over by me and watch me," said Jim. "Then you can try." So Penny stood by Jim and watched. She soon felt sure she could do what he did—but her little fingers were not nearly strong enough for milking and she gave it up. "Can I have a little milk for my lamb?" she asked. "It's time for his supper."

"No—you go and get some of the old milk from the kitchen," said Jim. "And keep your lamb by you—look at him nosing into that pail over there! My goodness, we don't want him emptying the pails as fast as we fill them!"

So off went Penny to the kitchen. "You know, Skippetty," she said, "I like lambs much better than cows! But please don't grow up too soon, will you? You won't be nearly so sweet when you are a sheep!"

CHAPTER X

FUN IN THE DAIRY

THE days were very busy at Willow Farm now. There was always something to do! The hens had to be fed and looked after, the eggs taken and counted, the cows had to be milked, and swedes had to be carted to and from their field. The milk has to be set in the dairy for cream—and butter had to be made!

The dairy was a lovely place, big, airy and cold. The floor was of stone, the walls and ceiling were white-washed, and all the shelves were of stone too. It was very cold in there when the wind was in the east or the north. In the summer it would be a lovely cool place—the coolest place on the farm!

The children's mother loved the dairy. She was glad when the cows came because now she would be able to make her own butter. The children were very curious about this. They longed to see exactly how butter was made.

"What is going to be done with all the milk from our cows?" asked Rory. "There will be gallons each day!"

"Well, some is to be sold, in big churns," said his father. "Some we shall keep for ourselves. Some we shall skim for cream, and sell the cream. The skim-milk will be given to the pigs, or the calves when we have any——and the rest we shall make into butter."

"It all sounds lovely," said Sheila. "Do we empty the warm milk straight into the milk-churns, Daddy?"

"Good gracious no!" said her father. "We can't send warm milk out—it would soon turn sour. It has to be cooled."

"How can we cool it?" asked Benjy. "There are all kinds of funny things in the dairy, Daddy—does one of them cool the milk?"

"Come and see, next time the milk is taken to the dairy," said his father. So all the children trooped into the cool white room to see what happened that evening.

"Do you see that box-like thing fixed to the wall over there?" said their mother. "That is a kind of refrigerator—a machine for making things cold. See this pipe running to it—it brings cold water to the refrigerator, which has many pipes to carry the ice-cold water."

Mother poured some milk into a big pan on the top of the machine. The milk ran over the cold pipes and then fell into the big milk-churn standing below. It was quite cool by then!

"That's clever," said Rory, pleased. "Now I suppose the cool milk in the churn is ready to be taken to the town to be sold, Mummy?"

"Yes, it is," said his mother. "And what we are going to use ourselves has been taken to Harriet in the kitchen."

"What's going to be done with these big pails full of creamy milk?" asked Penny, dipping her finger into the creamy surface of one and then licking it.

"Don't do that, Penny dear!" said her mother. "That milk is going to be made into butter. But alas—our separator hasn't arrived yet—so we must separate our milk and cream in the old-fashioned way, and wait until our separator comes when we can then do it much more quickly."

Mother put the creamy milk into big shallow pans, which were set on the cold stone shelves.

"What will the milk do now?" asked Benjy. "I suppose the cream will all come up to the top, as it did on our bottles at home."

"Yes," said his mother. "You know that light liquids always rise to the top of heavier ones—and as cream is lighter than milk, it will rise to the surface, if we leave it to do so."

"How long will it be before the cream has all risen to the top?" asked Penny. "Ten minutes? I want to make some butter from it!"

Everybody laughed. Penny was always so impatient and expected things to be done at once.

"Penny! Don't be silly!" said Mother. "It will take twenty-four hours!"

"Gracious! I can't wait and see it come all that time!" said Penny. "Can't we make the butter today then?"

"Oh no, Penny," said Rory. "We've got to get enough cream first, silly. There won't be enough cream from one lot of milk, will there, Mummy? We'll have to store it a bit and wait till we have enough to churn into butter."

So Penny had to be patient and wait until the next day to see the cream being skimmed and stored for the making of butter. The children loved seeing the rich yellow cream lying smoothly on the top of the pans. Penny dipped her finger in and wrinkled the cream—it was almost as stiff as treacle!

"Don't, Penny!" said Sheila. "Do keep your fingers out of things!"

Mother skimmed the lovely cream off very carefully. She put it into a big cool crock. It did look fine. Mother put a little into a jug too.

"What's that for?" asked Penny.

"For your porridge tomorrow morning!" said Mother. "Take it in to Harriet when you go."

"What's going to be done with the blue-looking milk that's left," said Sheila.

"That can go to the pigs when they come tomorrow," said Mother. "Calves love it too—but we haven't any yet. It is called skim-milk, because we have skimmed the cream off."

Just then there was a great commotion outside, and Jim appeared, carrying something that looked extremely heavy over his broad shoulder. It was well-packed up.

"Goodness! It's our separator!" cried Mother in delight. "Come and help to unpack it, everybody."

"Now we shan't have to wait ages for the cream to separate itself from the milk!" said Rory, pleased. "We can separate it in a few minutes."

Everyone wanted to see how the separator work. It looked a queer machine when it was unpacked. The main body of it was painted a bright clean red. On the top was a round pan. A big handle stood out from the side. Two pipes came out from the middle part. It really looked a most business-like machine.

Jim ran some water through the machine to clean it. "I reckon you can start it straightaway," he said. "It's a new machine, quite ready to use."

"Pour some fresh milk into the pan at the top, Rory," said Mother. So Rory poured some in, filling the pan full.

Then Sheila was allowed to turn the handle. "I feel as if I'm turning the handle of a barrel-organ!" she said. "I wouldn't be surprised if the separator played a tune!"

"Well, *I* would!" said her mother, with a laugh. "Go on turning, Sheila. Now children, watch those two pipes that come out at the front."

Everybody watched—and lo and behold, from the top pipe came out good thick yellow cream—and from the bottom pipe flowed the separated milk, free from any cream!

"Goodness—isn't that clever?" said Rory. "I see now why this machine is called a separator—it really does separate the milk from the cream. I suppose as the cream is the lighter of the two liquids, it always comes out of the higher pipe, and the milk comes out of the lower one because it is heavier."

"Yes," said Mother. "This clever little machine does

in a few minutes what it takes us quite a long time to do by hand!"

Rory swung open the front of the machine when all the milk was separated. It was very neat inside. The children loved to see how things worked, and they tried to follow out what happened. It wasn't very difficult.

"Well now," said Mother, "that is another lot of cream for us! Pour in some more milk, Rory. Penny, you can have a turn at playing the barrel-organ this time!"

It was lovely to watch the milk and the cream spurting out from the two pipes. The children begged to be allowed to take it in turns to do the separating each day, and their mother said yes, they could.

"It is all part of the work of the farm," she said. "So you may certainly do your share. But don't come to me and say you are tired of using the separator in a week's time, because I certainly shan't listen to you!"

The children couldn't imagine being tired of playing about with the separator. They were simply longing to use the butter-churn too, and see the butter being made.

Harriet was to make the butter, with Mother to help her. Harriet had been a dairy-maid before, and she was good at butter-making.

"You know, butter comes well with some folks and it doesn't come at all with others," she said, solemnly, to the children. "Now I'm going to make butter on Tuesdays and Saturdays so if anyone wants to help, they can come along to the dairy then."

"We'll all come!" said the children at once. "We're not going to miss doing a single thing at Willow Farm!"

CHAPTER XI

BUTTER—AND PIGS

ON the following Saturday Harriet bustled into the cool dairy. The sun poured down outside, for it was now mid-April, and spring was well on the way. But the dairy was as cool as ever.

In the big cold crock there was a great deal of cream. Harriet was going to turn it into golden butter. Penny peeped into the dairy with Skippetty behind her.

"Are you going to begin, Harriet?" she asked. "Shall I tell the others?"

"Yes," said Harriet, turning up her sleeves. "But just you leave that lamb of yours behind, please, Miss Penny! I never knew such a creature for poking its nose into things! It would gobble up all my precious cream as soon as look at it! You keep it out of the dairy. Do you know that it went into my larder this morning and nibbled the cheese?"

Penny giggled. Skippetty was a marvellous lamb, always doing the most unexpected things. She went to fetch the others. They came crowding into the dairy.

The butter-churn was in the middle. It was a funny-looking thing.

"It's just a strong barrel mounted on a framework of wood to hold it," said Rory. "And there's a handle to turn the barrel over and over and over."

"All hand-churns are like this," said Harriet. "This one's made of beech. The last one I had was made of oak —but I always say butter comes fastest in beech!"

Harriet poured the thick, yellow cream into the barrel-shaped churn. She fixed on the lid firmly. Then she took the handle and turned it strongly and regularly. The barrel at once turned over and over and over, swinging easily as it went.

"What a lovely noise the cream makes, splashing about inside!" said Sheila. They all listened. They could hear the cream being dashed about inside the churn.

"Why do you have to turn the churn over and over like that?" asked Benjy. "Is that the way to make the cream into butter? I know I once helped our cook to whip some cream for the top of a jelly, and after I had whipped it with a fork for a while it went all solid."

"Yes—cream goes solid when it is whipped," said Harriet, still turning the churn by the handle. Her face was red, and she looked hot.

"Let me have a turn," begged Sheila. "I could do it just as easily as you, Harriet."

All the children had a turn, though Penny found the churn heavy for her small arms. Harriet took the handle again, and soon she nodded her head.

"The butter's coming," she said. "I can feel it. The churn is heavier to turn."

"It's taken about twenty minutes," said Rory, looking at his watch. "I call that quick, Harriet—please take off the lid and let's look inside. I can't hear so much splashing now!"

So Harriet stopped churning and took off the lid. The children all peered inside. There was no thick cream to be seen! Instead there were lumps of yellow butter floating in some milky-looking liquid.

"That's the buttermilk that the butter is swimming about in," said Harriet. "Now a few more turns and I'll get out the butter!"

It was really exciting to see the butter forming like that from the cream. It seemed like magic to Penny. The children watched closely as Harriet poured away the buttermilk and then washed the lumps of butter till it was quite free from the milk.

She took up two flat wooden butter-handles and picked up the butter. She placed it all on a wooden tray, and then took the wooden butter-roller. With clever hands she pressed and rolled the butter till it was quite free of all moisture, and was firm and hard. Then neatly and deftly she made it into pound and half-pound pieces.

"There!" she said, wiping her hands on her apron. "Good rich butter, yellow and firm! Some to sell, some to eat. You shall have some for breakfast tomorrow morning!"

"Daddy is going to have paper wrapping printed to wrap our butter in when it's sold," said Sheila. "It is going to have 'Willow Farm Butter' printed on it. Oh dear—I shall feel so grand when I see that. Harriet, can we wrap the butter up when the new wrappings come?"

"If your hands are clean and you can wrap the butter neatly," said Harriet. "I'll show you how later on."

"Now we know how to separate cream from milk, and how to make butter from cream," said Penny, patting the wooden churn with her hand.

"I do think we are lucky," said Benjy, as they all left the cool dairy. "Our own eggs for breakfast—our own milk to drink—our own cream for porridge—and our own butter for our bread!"

"And I expect we shall have our own cheese too," said Rory. "Harriet says she can make cheese. She says she can make it from milk. She puts rennet into the milk and that separates the curds and the whey in the milk. Then she presses the curds, and they make cheese!"

"Gracious! It all sounds very easy," said Penny. "I shall help her when she does it."

The children were very happy. The weather was kind, the sun shone down warmly, and work on the farm went smoothly. The hens laid well, the cows gave splendid milk, and twice a week butter was made in the dairy.

The piglets were the next excitement. They arrived in a cart, squealing loudly! How they squealed! The children could not imagine what the noise was when they heard the cart coming slowly up the lane.

"Oh! It's the piglets!" yelled Benjy, and gave Scamper such a fright that the little squirrel shot up into a tree and would not come down for a long time. The children, with Skippetty the lamb behind them, rushed up the lane to meet the cart.

"The old mother-pig is there too," said Rory, in delight. "Gracious, what a giant she is! Oh, look at the piglets—aren't they sweet?"

All the children crowded round the pig-sty when the pig-family were put into it. The old sow grunted and lay down. The piglets scampered about busily.

"I simply *must* catch one and feel what it's like!" said Rory and he jumped down into the sty. He bent down to pick up a piglet—but it slipped away from him. He bent to get another—but that slipped away too. No matter how he tried he could *not* get hold of a piglet.

"They're all soft and silky and slippery!" he called to the others. "I can't possibly catch hold of one—they all slip off like eels!"

The others went into the sty to see if they could catch a piglet too, but to their surprise they found that it was just as Rory had said—the tiny creatures were far too slippery to hold!

They all went out of the sty a good deal more quickly than they went in! The sow didn't like to see them trying to catch her piglets, and she rose up in anger. She rushed at Rory and he only just got out of the way in time!

"Goodness! I didn't think she would be so fierce!" said Rory, rubbing his legs. "Isn't she ugly? But I like her all the same. Good old sow!"

"What's a father-pig called?" asked Penny.

"A boar," said Rory. "We haven't got a boar. But do you remember there was one at Cherry Tree Farm? He had a ring through his nose."

"Yes, why did he?" asked Penny. "I always meant to ask Uncle Tim and I never did."

"It's because pigs root about so," said Rory. "They try to root up the grass to get at any grubs or insects underneath, you know—and Uncle Tim didn't want his grass spoilt so he put a ring through the boar's nose."

"Well, I don't see how that stopped him from rooting about," said Penny.

"Well—would *you* like to go rooting up grass if Daddy put a ring through your nose?" asked Rory. "Wouldn't it hurt you every time you tried to nose up the grass?"

"Oh, I see," said Penny. "Yes, of course it would. Well, what about bulls? They have a ring through their noses too because I've seen them. And they don't go rooting up grass, do they?"

"No, they don't," said Rory. "But their ring isn't because of that, silly! It's so that they can be led by their nose, and not run away or get fierce, because if they try to pull away, their nose will be dreadfully hurt!"

The little pigs were really sweet. All the children loved them and begged to feed them each day. The big sow fed them herself for a while, but soon they grew big enough to want other food than her milk. Then the big trough was filled with food for them. How they loved it!

"Hie, little piglets, here is the butter-milk for you from our butter-making!" cried Rory. "And here is some whey from our cheese-making! And here is some separated milk from our cream-making!"

"And here are kitchen scraps!" cried Sheila, putting them into the trough. The little pigs squealed with excitement and rushed to the long wooden trough. There was plenty of room for them all, but they couldn't see that. They tried to push each other away to get at the food and made such a noise that the children laughed with glee.

"Oh look—three of them have got right into the trough itself!" cried Penny. "Oh you naughty little piglets! Get out of your dinner! Oh, how I would hate to eat dinner I was treading on!"

The pig-wash in the trough soon disappeared. The piglets loved it. They grew fat and round and big. The sow ate well too. She loved little potatoes and the children often brought her a meal of these, or of potato parings.

"I really believe the old sow would eat anything!" said Rory, as he watched her gobble up enormous mouthfuls. "I don't wonder we have a saying 'As greedy as a pig!'"

"What about the saying 'As dirty as a pig'," said Sheila. "People always seem to think that pigs are dirty animals. But our sow is beautifully clean—and so are her dear little piglets."

"It depends on how they are kept," said Jim, who was passing by with the cows. "If pig-sties aren't regularly cleaned out of course the pigs will be dirty. How can they help it, poor creatures? Now, your sty has a good run, and it is cleaned out well—so your pigs are clean and healthy. Maybe you'll let them run on grass a bit later on. They'll love that."

Jim was right. The piglets and the sow had the run of the orchard, and they were very happy. They ran and squealed and really enjoyed themselves. Skippetty often went to join them, and once he jumped on the side of the old sow when she was lying down basking in the sun.

But he didn't do it again! The old sow was very angry, and she ran all round the orchard after Skippetty till he was quite frightened!

"Skippetty, you must behave yourself!" said Penny. "Come with me, and don't worry the sow any more! Keep out of mischief for an hour or two!"

But the lamb couldn't be good for long. He went into the hen-house and began to nibble at the box of broken oyster-shell there! How Penny laughed!

"Look, Benjy! Look, Rory!" she called. "Skippetty wants to lay eggs with hard shells. He's nibbling the

Skippetty had to run for his life!

broken oyster-shell in the hen-house! Whatever will he do next!"

Nobody knew—but nobody minded, for who could help loving a black-faced, skippetty lamb?

CHAPTER XII

OUT IN THE FIELDS

AROUND the farmhouse lay great fields, sloping gently down the hill. Most of the fields were bordered by little brooks, whose sides were set with willows. The fields all had names, and Penny liked to chant them in a kind of song.

"Long Meadow, Top Field, Green Meadow, Swing Field, Long Bottom, Brook's Lea, Holtspur!"

All these places were fields of different shapes and sizes. The children soon knew every one. They had all been ploughed in the autumn, and Rory wished that he had been able to watch the plough at work.

"I've always wanted to guide a plough," he said, longingly. "I wanted to help with the ploughing last autumn when we were at Cherry Tree Farm—but Uncle Tim wouldn't let me."

"Why do fields have to be ploughed?" asked Penny. "It seems a waste of time to me to turn up a field and furrow it!"

"We'll ask Tammylan. There he comes!" said Rory, waving to the wild man, who was coming along beside the hedge nearby. He often came to see them, and told them tales about the different animals and birds he knew so well.

"Tammylan! How's the hare?" yelled Penny, as soon as she saw him.

"Much better," said Tammylan. "His legs have mended—but he limps now. Still, he can get along quite fast. I think he will live with me in my cave though. He seems to be rather afraid of going along into the fields unless I am with him."

"I wish I had a hare to live with *me*," said Penny.

"Well, you've got a lamb," said Benjy. "That's more than enough, surely. Do you know, Tammylan, Skippetty ate Jim's lunch yesterday? It was cheese, and Skippetty found it and ate it. Jim was awfully cross. I had to get him some of our home-made cheese from Harriet."

"That lamb sounds more like a goat to me," said Tammylan, with a laugh. "Goats eat everything and anything, you know. I once had one that ate books out of bookshelves!"

"Tammylan—why do fields have to be ploughed?" asked Rory. "I know that gardens have to be dug—and I suppose ploughing is a quick way of digging a big field."

"Yes," said Tammylan. "We couldn't dig over our enormous fields! We plough up the ground because we want the rain and air and frost to get to it, Rory. Let's come and look at the plough over there in the shed."

They all went to look at it. Tammylan pointed out the big steel blade or share that was pushed into the earth when the plough was dragged along by the horses.

"That great steel blade cuts a big slice of earth," he said. "Then it is turned over. Now look at this smaller blade at the side of the plough. That's called a coulter, and it cuts the straight edge of the furrow."

"The ploughman holds the handles of the plough, doesn't he?" said Penny, taking hold of them, and pretending to guide the plough. "Oh, I'm sure I could plough!"

"Yes—you could plough!" said Tammylan, a twinkle in his eye. "But you wouldn't be able to plough *straight*!"

"I've watched the ploughman often," said Benjy. "He keeps the plough awfully straight, so that the furrows lie quite straight too, close to one another. At Uncle Tim's farm a boy sometimes guided the horses—he walked at their heads and led them. Perhaps Jim would let *me* do that this autumn when he ploughs the fields again."

"Daddy says he isn't going to have his plough drawn by horses this autumn," said Sheila. "He is going to have a tractor."

"What's that?" asked Penny, surprised.

"Oh, it's a kind of little engine driven by petrol or oil," said Sheila. "It can be fastened in front of the plough instead of horses, can't it, Tammylan? Daddy says he will get a tractor with caterpillar wheels."

"Whatever for?" asked Penny. "It will be like a tank then!"

"Well, our fields are rather soft," said Sheila, proud that she knew so much about it, "and Daddy says that caterpillar wheels prevent the tractor from sinking into the soil. I say—won't it be fun to see a tractor going! I do hope we can take turns at driving it!"

"Look!" cried Rory, suddenly. "What's Jim getting out of the shed over there?"

They all looked. "It's a cultivator." said Tammylan. "Ah now we shall see a little hard work done on this field!"

Jim was dragging out a big iron frame on wheels. Below it were long steel teeth. Jim did not let them touch the ground until he reached the field where he was going to work. Darling, one of the big farm horses, dragged the cultivator for him, and Jim got into the seat of the machine.

Soon he was at work. Darling plodded along the furrowed field steadily, her head well down as she went uphill. Jim let down the steel teeth of the cultivator with a click. They bit into the good soil.

"Look how it's raking it all thoroughly!" cried Sheila, pleased. "It's breaking up the furrows and smashing up the earth into tiny bits. It will be all ready for seed-sowing when Jim has finished!"

"Ploughed fields have to be harrowed to make them ready for the seeds," said Tammylan. "Get out of the way, Penny—Jim will harrow you if you don't look out!"

But Penny wanted to stop Jim. He pulled up Darling with a jerk. "Jim! Let me sit on the seat and see what it feels like!" shouted Penny. Jim grinned. He had a soft spot in his heart for small Penny. He got down and lifted her up in the big brown seat. He clicked to the horse and the cultivator moved forward. Penny would have been jerked right off the seat if Jim had not been holding her tightly!

"Oh!" she said. "It's a very hard, jerky seat, isn't it, Jim?"

"I don't notice it!" said Jim, as he climbed back and clicked to Darling.

"Jim! What's going to be planted in this field?" cried Benjy, as the cultivator moved off with a clanking noise.

"Clover!" shouted back Jim. "I'll be sowing it on Friday if you want to watch! And there'll be wheat in Long Bottom."

The children remembered seeing pictures of people walking down a field, casting out seed first on one side and then from the other.

"I could help Jim sow the clover," said Penny. "I could bring my basket and tie it in front of me and put the seed there. I should like to walk down the field throwing seed first from one hand and then from the other."

"Well, it won't be quite like that!" said Tammylan. "Now come along, children—if you want to show me the new piglets, you'll have to show me now. My visit is only a short one this time!"

"Well, will you come again on Friday and watch us all sowing seeds?" begged Penny, slipping her hand in Tammylan's big brown one. "Do come, Tammylan. It will be such fun."

"I'll come if you can tell me the answer to the puzzle I set you about horses and cows!" said Tammylan, with a laugh. "Now Penny—do a horse and cow get up from the grass in exactly the same way?"

"Oh, I know the answer to *that*!" said Penny. "I've watched all our cows and horses—and Tammylan, it's so funny, cows get up on their hind-legs first and kneel on their front legs—but horses do it the other way. They throw out their front legs first and then raise themselves on their hind-legs! So I know the answer to that puzzle you see—and you'll have to come on Friday!"

"Good girl," said Tammylan. "Yes—I'll come on Friday—and we'll see whether we sow seed or not!"

"Well, of course we shall," said Penny, puzzled.

But Penny was wrong! When Friday came the children all went to Top Meadow, hoping to meet Jim there and be given seed to sow. But Jim was taking Darling into the field and behind her was a curious affair. It was like a very long narrow box raised on wheels. The children stared.

"What's that, Jim?" asked Sheila, puzzled.

"It's a broadcast sower," said Jim. "Watch me put my clover seed into it!"

"Oh—is *that* going to sow the seed instead of you?" asked Benjy, deeply disappointed. "I thought we could all help to sow the seed. Oh look—there's Tammylan, grinning all over his face. Tammylan! I believe you knew we wouldn't help with the sowing today!"

"Well, I did have a sort of an idea that we should have to watch Jim!" said Tammylan. "Anyway, it's very interesting. Let's see what happens."

Jim had emptied half a sack of fine clover seed into the long narrow box. He shut down the lid. Then he set off down the field, with all the children watching carefully.

"Oh look—the seed is falling from holes at the bottom of the long narrow box!" cried Sheila. Sure enough it was—it fell steadily and evenly over the field, and sowed the field in a fair quicker way than if the children had done it by hand.

"Are you going to sow the wheat with the broadcast sower too?" asked Rory, when Jim came by again.

"No," said Jim. "I'm sowing that with the seed drill this afternoon. You'll like to see that. It's a cleverer thing than this because the drill makes the furrows, sows the seed evenly, and then covers it up with soil!"

Tammylan stayed to lunch with the children that day. He told them about a robin that had built its nest inside one of his old shoes at the back of the cave!

"When the eggs hatch out I shall have plenty of company!" he said. "The young robins will be very tame. I don't know how they will get on with the hare, but I've no doubt they will all be friends in no time."

That afternoon they all went to see the seed drill planting the wheat. This was a bigger thing than the broadcast sower. The seed was carried in a kind of tank, and then passed from there into tubes. These pipes entered the soil a little way below the surface and dropped the seeds there.

"That *is* a good idea," said Rory, as they watched the seed drill start off down Long Bottom Field. "It sows the seed under the surface, all at the same depth—and then neatly covers it up so that the birds can't get it!"

Jim went halfway down the field with the seed drill and then stopped. He did something to the drill, and then set off again.

"What was the matter, Jim?" asked Penny, as Jim came up the field by the children again.

"The drill was sowing the seed too thickly," said Jim. "I adjusted the drill so that the seed didn't come out so fast. It's about right now, I think."

Penny ran beside him when the other children went off with Tammylan.

"The fields have been ploughed and harrowed and sown!" she panted. "What else is there to be done, Jim?

It seems to me that fields take as much looking after as animals and hens!"

"Oh they do!" said Jim, guiding the drill round a corner. "But now I can take a rest from working in them for a while, Miss Penny! They've got to look after themselves a bit now—and the sun and the rain will work for me! I must wait now till the clover is grown and the wheat is ready to cut! Ah, then we'll be busy again. Harvesting is as busy a time as spring!"

CHAPTER XIII

A LITTLE EXCITEMENT FOR SHEILA

THE weeks went by, and the four children were sad when their holidays came to an end. Then they all went walking across the fields to the rectory, and there, with three other children, they had lessons. But always they looked longingly out of the window, wondering what their hens were doing, what Scamper was doing, if Skippetty was in mischief, and whether the three dogs were helping Davey with the sheep.

How they raced home after school! Saturdays and Sundays were whole holidays, and if they had worked hard they were allowed Wednesday afternoon off as well. So they could still help a good deal, and Sheila could manage her hens very well.

Skippetty hated to see Penny going off each morning without him. He bleated after her most piteously, and the little girl begged to be allowed to take him. But Mother always said no, most firmly.

But Skippetty was determined to be like the lamb in the nursery rhyme, and one day he managed to squeeze through a gap in the hedge and trot after Penny to school.

The children were quite a good way off, but Skippetty could hear their voices far ahead and he followed them eagerly.

Just as the children got to the Rectory they turned and saw Skippetty!

"Oh! Penny had a little lamb
That followed her to school!"

shouted the children in delight. The rector came to the door and laughed.

"Well, like Mary's lamb, I'm afraid it's against the rule," he smiled. "Penny, take the lamb to the apple orchard and shut it in."

But Penny couldn't have shut the gate properly because the lamb got out and went to the schoolroom door. The children saw the door open just a little—and then they saw Skippetty's black, blunt nose appearing round the edge!

They squealed with laughter, and Skippetty was frightened and ran back to the orchard. This time Rory was sent to see that he was safe, and the lamb was seen no more in school that morning.

Scamper *was* allowed to come, because he was quite content to wait for Benjy in the trees outside. Scamper was a little restless now that spring had really come. He sometimes went off for a day or two to the woods, and Benjy missed him terribly then. But he always came back. Once he came back in the middle of the night, and jumped in at Benjy's little window under the thatch. Benjy got a shock when Scamper landed on his middle and ran up to his face!

Fanny was a great help with the hens. She always did them if Sheila was kept late at school, and she and Sheila kept the egg-book with enormous pride.

"Fancy—over four hundred eggs already!" said Fanny, proudly, counting them up in the book. "Miss Sheila, a hen is supposed to lay about two hundred and twenty eggs a year, if it is a good layer—but it looks as if ours will each lay far more than that."

Then there came a week when there were not so many eggs—and one night when Sheila went to shut up her hens she found that there was one missing!

"Fanny!" she called. "There are only nineteen hens and one cock. What's happened to the other hen?"

"I can't think," said Fanny. "She must be somewhere about. Oh, I do hope she's not wandered away too far and been stolen. There have been gypsies in that field over there this week—maybe they've taken her."

The girls called Benjy, Rory and Penny, and they all began to hunt for the lost hen. It was Penny who found her!

The little girl had hunted all round the orchard and in the hedges of the fields. As a last hope she went into the farm-garden. There was a big clump of rhododendron bushes there, and Penny pushed her way into the middle of them.

And there, sitting quietly down by herself, was the lost brown hen! She looked up at Penny when the little girl came near, and gave a quiet cluck as if to say "Hallo! Don't disturb me. I'll all right!"

"Oh, Sheila, I've found the hen, I've found her!" yelled Penny. "Shall I bring her? She's here under the rhododendron bush!"

"No, I'll come and get her, don't touch her!" shouted back Sheila, who hated anyone to touch her precious hens. She ran into the garden and went to the clump of rhododendrons. She pushed them aside and looked at the hen.

"Oh you naughty Fluffy!" she said. "Why didn't you come to bed when I shut up all the rest tonight?"

She lifted up the hen—and then she and Penny gave a yell. "She's sitting on eggs! Look, she's sitting on eggs!"

Sure enough, in a neat cluster, were eleven nice brown

eggs! The hen clucked and struggled as Sheila lifted her off the eggs.

"Oh! No wonder the eggs have been short the last day or two!" said Sheila. "And I do believe you must have stayed away for three or four nights out here, you bad hen! I haven't been counting you all as I should, because I felt sure you came when you were called. Well, well—what shall we do with you?"

Fanny was pleased and excited. "We'll put her and her eggs into a coop," she said. "We'll give her two more We'll have our own chicks now. Miss Sheila. Oh, that *will* be fun!"

So the clucking hen was given a nice coop for herself, and her eggs were put neatly under her—thirteen now—and she settled on them happily, near the hen-house. Everyone went to see her every day. She looked out at them from the coop, and gave little clucks.

Each morning Sheila lifted her off the eggs, and gave her a good meal of corn and fresh water.

"Don't let her be off too long," said Fanny. "If the eggs get cold they won't hatch and we won't have our chicks."

So Sheila timed the hen each day, and gave her exactly twenty minutes off her eggs and no more. She felt the eggs just before the hen went back, and they were quite warm.

"Twenty-one days she's got to sit," said Fanny. "But of course we don't exactly know when she began."

"Do you know, Fanny, there's a hen that sits all day in one of the nesting-boxes, and never lays an egg!" said Sheila, a few days later. "It is most annoying of her. I keep shooing her out, but she always goes back."

"Well, that means she wants to sit on a nest of eggs and hatch out chickens just as old Fluffy is doing," said Fanny. "Oh, Miss Sheila—my uncle has a clutch of duck's eggs. I wonder if your father would like to buy them, and let the hen sit on them! Then we'd have ducklings!"

"But do hens sit on duck's eggs?" asked Penny, who was listening. "Won't the hen know they are not hen's eggs?"

"Of course she won't know!" said Sheila. "How could she? Oh, Fanny, that would be fun! I'll ask Daddy straightaway."

Sheila's father gave her the money to buy the duck's eggs. She and Fanny went to get them. Sheila liked them very much.

"What a pretty greeny colour they are!" she said. "They are bigger than hen's eggs too. Fanny, don't ducks sit on their own eggs? Why must we give them to a hen to sit on?"

"Well, ducks aren't very good mothers," said Fanny. "They leave their eggs too long—and sometimes they get tired of sitting and desert them. But a hen is a good mother and nearly always hatches out her eggs."

The thirteen duck's eggs were put into a coop, and the broody hen was put over them. She got up and down a few times, and then settled on them quite happily. All the children watched with interest while she made up her mind.

"Goodness! We'll have twenty-six new birds soon!" said Benjy pleased.

"Oh no!" said Fanny. "You hardly ever get thirteen chicks from thirteen eggs! Maybe one or two are bad you know, and won't hatch. We'll be lucky if we get twelve out of the thirteen."

"Will they hatch out at the same time?" asked Penny.

"No," said Fanny. "Duck's eggs take twenty-eight days to hatch, you know—a week more than a hen's. I love little ducklings. They waddle so—and my word, when they first go into the water, you should see how upset the hen is! She thinks they are her own chicks, not somebody else's ducklings, you see! And she knows that water's not good for chicks, so she gets into an awful state when they waddle off to the pond!"

"Oh, I shall like to see that!" said Penny.

The two hens were very contented and happy sitting on their eggs. Each day they were lifted off and given a good meal and fresh water. Penny told the others that she had seen the hens turning their eggs over so that they were warmed evenly on both sides. She thought that was very clever of them.

Then there came the exciting day when the first chicks hatched out! Penny heard the hen clucking and she ran across to the coop. She saw a bit of broken egg-shell—and then she saw a yellow chick peeping out from beneath the mother hen. She ran squealing to the house in excitement.

"Come quickly, come quickly! The chicks are hatching out!"

The others ran to see. But only one chick had hatched out so far. The hen kept putting her head on one side as if she could hear more chicks getting ready to break their shell. The children were so thrilled.

One more chick hatched out before they had to go off to school. That was a yellow one too. They begged to be allowed to stay and see all the eggs hatching out but their mother shook her head.

"No," she said. "The eggs were not all set at the same time, because the hen laid them herself. It may be tomorrow or the next day when they all hatch out."

So the children had to wait in patience—but at last all but two of the egg-shells were empty, and eleven little chicks scampered about the coop.

"These two won't hatch," said Fanny, picking up the last two eggs. "They are addled. Well—eleven isn't bad—and good healthy chicks they look!"

The chicks were given nothing at all to eat for the first twenty-four hours—then Fanny showed Sheila what to give them—a scattering of bread and oatmeal crumbs, and a tiny saucer of water. They soon pecked up the food and cheeped in little high voices for more.

Everybody loved them. Some were all yellow, as bright as buttercups. Some were yellow and black, and one was all black. The mother-hen was very pleased with them. She soon took them about the yard and showed them how to scratch for food.

When she found a titbit she called loudly to her chicks and they all came running at once. She shared it with them, which the children thought was very nice of her.

"She's a real proper mother," said Penny. "Just like ours!"

When one of the stable cats came into the yard the hen called to her chicks in quite a different voice. They heard the warning in her clucks and ran to her at once. If she was in the coop they got under her wings and breast-feathers, and not one could be seen! Then, when the danger was past and the cat had gone, first one little yellow head, then another and another would poke up from the hen's feathers and look out with bright beady eyes.

That made the children laugh. "The hen has a dozen heads!" cried Benjy. "Doesn't she look funny!"

The duck's eggs hatched out some time later. The children were glad because it was a Saturday and they could watch everything from beginning to end.

The little ducks uncurled themselves from the eggshells and stood on unsteady feet. They fluffed themselves out and the children looked at them in amazement.

"How *could* those ducks ever have got into the eggs?" cried Sheila. "They look twice as big already!"

The children liked the ducks even better than the chicks. They were so funny as they waddled about the yard. They were not so obedient as the chicks, and the mother hen had a lot of trouble with them.

Then the day came when they all wanted to go to the duck-pond! They had wandered quite near the edge of it, and suddenly one little duck felt that it simply MUST splash in that lovely water! So it waddled off, while the mother hen stood still in horror and clucked for it to come back.

But to her annoyance the other ducklings also ran off to join the first one—and then, with little splashes and cheeps of delight every duckling slid or fell into the water and sailed off in excitement on the pond!

The mother hen went nearly mad with worry. She rushed about beside the pond, clucking and calling, while the other hen with her chicks stood looking on in horror. The ducklings had a wonderful time on the water and took no notice at all of their mother hen's scolding when they came out.

"Cheep, cheep," they said to one another. "That was fine! We'll do it again! Cheep, cheep!"

"Don't you worry so much, old mother-hen," said Sheila, sorry for the fluffy brown bird. "Your chicks are not chicks—they are ducklings! Can't you see the difference?"

But the hen couldn't! She worried herself dreadfully every time the ducklings took to the water—and then she grew tired of them and left them to themselves. She joined the hens in the yard, and scratched about contentedly, laying eggs again, and forgetting all about the naughty family of chicks that had so unexpectedly turned into ducklings!

The other mother-hen taught her chicks all that they should know, and then she too left them to themselves. They were quite content to run about together, scratching in the ground, and pecking at the cabbage stalks with the bigger hens. But the children did not like them nearly as much as they grew.

"They're leggy and skinny," said Benjy. "They're not so pretty. I like hens to be either hens or chicks. I don't like them in-between!"

But Sheila and Fanny were proud of their young

chickens, and entered them in the egg-book. "Eleven chicks, twelve ducklings." That was a real feather in their caps, to have twenty-three birds more than they had started with!

CHAPTER XIV

THE WONDERFUL SHEEP-DOGS

PENNY often went to see Davey the shepherd. She took Skippetty with her and the lamb was very funny with the other sheep. It seemed to turn up its little black nose at them, and to think itself much too grand to frisk about with the lambs!

"It nibbles the grass now, Davey," said Penny. "It doesn't want nearly so much milk. And oh, it does eat such a lot of things it shouldn't!"

"It's like its mistress then!" said Davey with a laugh, for he knew that Penny loved picking off the unripe gooseberries, and liked sucking the tubes out of the clover heads. "Now, Tuppenny, you've come at the right moment this afternoon! I'm going to take the sheep from this hill to the next—and you can see Rascal, Nancy and Tinker at work if you like!"

"Oh, I *would* like!" cried Penny in delight. "May I go and tell the others, Davey? They'd so like to watch too."

"Well, hurry then," said Davey. "I'll give you ten minutes—then I must set the dogs to work."

It was Wednesday afternoon, and the four children had a half-holiday. Sheila had meant to give the hen-house a good clean. Rory had said he would work in the fields and Benjy had meant to help his mother in her farm-garden, where lettuces and onions, carrots and beans were all coming up well.

But when they heard that the sheep-dogs were to be set to work to help the shepherd, they all of them changed their minds at once!

"Golly! We *must* go and see that," said Rory, and he rushed to tell Jim that he would finish his work in the fields after tea. In ten minutes' time all four children were up on the hill with Davey.

He smiled at them, his grey eyes twinkling. "It's marvellous how quick children can be when they want to do anything!" he said, "and wonderful how slow they are when they have to do something they don't like. Now look—I want my sheep taken to the sheltered slope you can see on the next hill. They've got to cross over three of your streams, two of which only have narrow plank bridges—but my dogs will take them all safely without any help from me!"

"But Davey—aren't you going with them?" asked Penny, in surprise.

"No, little Tuppenny, I'm not!" said Davey. "I just want you to see how clever my dogs can be. Ah, you should see old Rascal at the sheep-dog trials! My word, he's a wonder! He can round up strange sheep and take them anywhere quicker than any other dog. I tell you, he's worth his weight in gold, that dog!"

The four children stood on the sunny hillside, eager to see what was going to happen. Davey whistled to his dogs. They came running up, two of them beautiful collies, the third a mongrel.

"Round them up, boys," said Davey, and he waved his arms towards the sheep grazing peacefully on the hillside. "Take them yonder!" He waved his arms towards the next hill.

The dogs stared at him with wagging tails. Then they bounded off swiftly. They ran to the sheep and made them leave their grazing. The sheep, half-frightened, closed in together. One or two took no notice of the dogs, but

Rascal ran so close to their heels that they too had to join the others.

"Sheep always flock when anything troubles them," said Davey. "Now watch those silly little lambs!"

Some of the lambs, instead of joining the sheep, had run away down the hillside. Tinker went after them, and very cleverly headed them back. As soon as a lamb seemed to be running away again, Tinker was there, close beside it, and it found that it had to go with the others!

"Goodness! I wish I was a sheep-dog!" said Penny. "I'd like to make the sheep do what I told them!"

Soon the sheep were in a bunch together, with the three dogs running round them. Davey waved his arms. That was the signal for the dogs to begin guiding the sheep to the next hill.

In a trice the sheep were set running downhill. Rascal ran round and round the flock, keeping it together. He didn't bark once. Nancy helped him. Tinker kept in front, making the leading sheep go the right way. It was marvellous to see how he made them keep to the path he wanted.

They came to a stream, too broad for the sheep to jump and too deep to wade. A narrow plank bridge ran from side to side. The leading sheep did not want to cross it. They ran along the bank, bleating.

It took Rascal half a minute to get them back to the bridge. But still they wouldn't cross.

"He can't make them!" cried Benjy, excited. "The sheep are too stupid!"

"Oh, the stupider they are, the easier," said Davey. "It's the ones that try to think for themselves that are the most difficult to manage. The ones that don't think, but just blindly follow the others, are very easy indeed. But watch Rascal he can't be beaten by a few silly sheep! There—look—he's got one on to the bridge!"

How Rascal had got the first sheep there nobody quite knew. The dog seemed to go in and out and round about the sheep till it found itself on the bridge! It couldn't go backwards, because Rascal was just behind it—so it had to go forward!

Once one sheep had crossed the others felt they must follow! Rascal leapt off the bridge and stood close beside it. Tinker stood the other side. Nancy kept the sheep together behind, forcing them forwards to the bridge.

It was marvellous to watch. The dogs worked together beautifully, never letting a sheep get away, and making them all go over the bridge as quietly as possible.

The sheep were sure-footed, and trotted easily over the narrow plank. Penny was afraid that one of the lambs might fall in, but of course not one lost its footing.

"Sheep are really mountain animals," said Davey. "I used to keep them in Wales on the mountainside. Some of the hills there were so rocky and steep that I couldn't get near the sheep—but they leapt from rock to rock and didn't slip once. So a narrow bridge like that means nothing to them!"

All the sheep passed over the bridge. Rascal leapt ahead of the flock and turned them to the left instead of to the right. Nancy brought up the stragglers. Tinker ran round the flock. They all went on to the next stream, where a little stone bridge was built across.

The sheep went over without any difficulty. "They know by now that the dogs are taking them somewhere," said Davey. "They don't like leaving the hill where they have been for many weeks, but they will soon get used to new grazing."

Just then the dogs paused and looked back to the hillside they had left. They had come to a forking of the hill-paths, and were not sure which one to take—to the east or to the west.

Davey knew what they wanted. He waved his arm and gave a shrill whistle. "That means I want the sheep taken to the west side of the hill," he told the children. "Watch how the dogs understand me!"

The dogs had hardly seen Davey wave and heard his

whistle before they headed the sheep towards the west! The children were amazed.

"Why, it's as if they were men," said Rory. "Though men couldn't run around the sheep as quickly as the dogs. But they understand just as we do. Oh Davey, you couldn't do without your dogs, could you?"

"No shepherd could," said Davey. "We depend on our dogs more than on anything else. Why, once when I was ill for two days, those dogs of mine looked after the sheep for me just as if I was out on the hills with them. Sharp as needles they are, and think for themselves just as much as you do!"

"Are they born as clever as all that?" asked Rory.

"Oh, sheep-dogs are always clever," said Davey, "but they have to be trained. I train them a little, but the other dogs teach a pup much more than I can by just letting him run around with them and see what they do. Some sheep-dogs are cleverer than others, just as some children are sharp and others are not. I can tell in a few months if a pup is going to be a good sheep-dog or not."

The sheep were made to cross another stream and then they were allowed to scatter on the western side of the hill. The dogs lay down, panting and tired. They had run many miles, because they had had to tear round and round the flock so many times! The sheep dropped their heads and began pulling at the short grass with enjoyment. It was good to be out there on the hillside in the sun, with new grass to eat!

"The dogs will stay with them till I come," said Davey. "Well—what do you think of them? Pretty sharp, aren't they?"

The shepherd was very proud of his dogs, and the children were too. "I think they're marvellous," said Rory. "I wish I had a flock of sheep and dogs like that!"

"Do you know, one winter's day two sheep got lost in a snowstorm," said Davey. "I reckoned I'd never get them again—but old Rascal there, he went out in the snow—and he brought back those sheep six hours later!"

"Did he really?" said Benjy astonished. "But how could he find them in the snow? Was it deep?"

"Yes," said the shepherd. "I counted the sheep and told Rascal that two were gone—and off he went. He must have hunted all up the hills and down before he found them. He was so tired when he got here that he couldn't even eat his supper! He just lay down with his head on my foot and fell fast asleep! Ah, he's a good dog that!"

"Well, thank you Davey, for letting us watch what your dogs can do," said Sheila. "Please tell us when they do anything else exciting!"

"You must come and watch the sheep-shearing in a fortnight's time," said Davey. "And when we dip the sheep you'll like to see that too. I'll let you know when to come!"

The children ran off down the hill. "Aren't there exciting things to do on a farm!" cried Penny, as she skipped along just like Skippetty the lamb. "Oh, how glad I am that we've left London and come to Willow Farm, Willow Farm, Willow Farm!"

CHAPTER XV

THE SHEARERS ARRIVE

ONE day three strange men appeared at the farm. The children looked at them in surprise, for they met them just as they were going off to school.

"Is your father about?" asked one of the men. "Well, tell him we're the shearers, will you?"

"I say! The sheep are going to be sheared!" cried

Rory. "Oh golly—if only we could stay home today and watch!"

"You'll see plenty, young sir," said the shearer, with a smile. "We'll be at work all day long, till night falls. We don't stop—once we're on the job!"

Rory flew off to tell his father. The four children watched the men being taken to one of the big open sheds.

"So that's where the sheep are to be sheared!" said Benjy. "I saw the shed being cleared yesterday, and I wondered why. I shall simply *tear* home from school today to watch."

"Do the shearers cut off all the poor sheep's wool?" asked Penny, feeling quite sad for the sheep. "Poor things—they *will* be cold!"

"Well, they're jolly hot now, in this sunny weather!" said Rory. "How would you like to wear a heavy woolly coat to go to school in this morning, Penny? I guess you'd be begging and begging us to let you take it off!"

Penny looked down at her short cotton frock. "Well, I'm hot even in this," she said, "and I should *melt* if I wore a woolly coat like the sheep. I expect they will be glad, after all."

"Of course they will!" said Sheila. "But they *will* look funny afterwards! I expect they feel funny too—all sort of undressed."

When the children came back from school that morning, they found the air full of the noise of bleating! The mother sheep had been separated from their lambs, and each was bleating for the other! What a noise it was!

"Look—they have driven the sheep into hurdles in the field near the shearing-shed," said Rory. "Last year's lambs are with them—but not this year's babies. So Skippetty won't lose his nice little woolly coat, Penny!"

"I'm glad," said Penny. "I don't want him all shaven and shorn! He's sweet as he is."

The dogs had had a busy morning bringing in the sheep

for the shearers. They had had to collect them from the hills, and bring them all back to the farm. They had worked hard and well, and Davey was pleased with them.

The shearers sat in the open shed. The sheep that had already been sheared had been set free and stood in a small flock, with Tinker on guard. He was to take them to the hills to graze as soon as another dozen or so sheep were ready.

The children ran to see exactly what happened. The farm felt busy that day—men hurried here and there with sheep, and the children's father gave loud orders. It was fun!

Rory watched the first shearer. A big sheep was taken up to him. Very deftly the sheep's legs were tied together so that it could not move. It might hurt itself if it struggled and got cut by the clippers.

Then the shearer got to work with his clippers. The children thought he was marvellous. He clipped the sheep's wool so that it came off like a big coat! Snip snip snip, went the clippers, and the wool was sheared off swiftly and cleanly. How queer the sheep began to look as its wool fell away from its skin!

The shearer looked up and smiled at the watching children.

"Are you my next customers?" he asked. "I've done nineteen sheep already today. One of you going to be the twentieth?"

"We're not sheep!" said Penny, indignantly.

"Dear me, so you're not!" said the shearer. He twisted the sheep he was doing so that he could shear the wool from its back. The wool fell away neatly.

"The wool's dirty," said Rory. "And it smells!"

"Well, these sheep haven't been made to swim through water," said the shearer. "If they are sent swimming a week or two before they are sheared, their fleeces are cleaner. Washed wool is worth more money. On the other hand, it doesn't weigh so much as unwashed, so there's not much in it!"

"What's the biggest number of sheep you have sheared in a day?" asked Benjy, who was longing to try his hand at clipping too.

"Sixty-eight," said the shearer. "But they were small ones. The bigger the sheep the longer it takes to shear it. I like shearing fat sheep the best—they are easiest of all to shear."

"Why?" asked Rory, surprised. "I should have thought it would have been difficult to get round them!"

"Well, you see," said the shearer, "a fat sheep's wool rises up well from the skin and makes it easy to shear. It's skin is oilier than a lean sheep's, and the oil makes the wool rise nicely. Wait till the shepherd brings along a really fat sheep and you'll see what I mean."

The shearer nearby was shearing the year-old lambs. They hated the shearing and bleated piteously.

"Are they being hurt?" asked Penny, anxiously.

"Not a bit!" said the shearer. "Sheep hate two things—one is being sheared, and the other is being dipped."

"*Dipped!*" said Rory. "What do you mean, dipped?"

"Oh, you'll see soon enough," said the man. "Davey here will show you one day soon!" He finished his lamb and sent it away with a smack. "These shearlings are quick to do," he said. "Their coats are not so thick as the big sheep's."

"Is a shearling a yearling?" asked Benjy.

"That's right," said the man, and took another shearling to clip. It was wonderful to see how quickly he clipped away the wool.

As each sheep was finished, and stood up, bare and frightened, Jim daubed its back with tar, and then sent it off to Tinker.

"What are you doing that for?" asked Benjy.

"Marking the sheep with your father's mark," said Jim.

"Then if the sheep happens to wander, the mark is known and the sheep are sent back."

The children looked at the mark. It was a big crooked letter W.

"W for Willow Farm," said Penny. "Oh—now we shall always know our own sheep!"

Jim rolled each fleece up tightly and tied it together. He threw it into a corner of the shed.

"They will all be packed into sacks and sold," he said. "It looks as if your father will do well this year with his wool. It's good wool, and weighs very heavy."

"Oh, I'm glad," said Rory. "I know he wants to buy some new farm-machinery, and he said if the sheep did well he would be able to. We've had lots of lambs, and not one of them has died. Skippetty was the only weakly one, and as soon as Penny took him for a pet, he began to grow big and fat."

"I notice he doesn't come into the shearing shed!" said Jim, with a grin. "I reckon he's afraid he will lose his nice little coat if he does!"

Skippetty was keeping well out of the way. He didn't like all the noise of bleating and crying. When the clipped sheep came out from the shed Skippetty looked at them in amazement. What were these curious-looking creatures? He didn't like them at all!

The sheep certainly did look queer when they ran back to the fields, shaven and shorn. They looked so small without their thick woolly coats. They felt cold too, but the month was warm, and they would take no harm. The shearing was never done when the winds were cold—only when it seemed as if the weather was going to hold fine and sunny and warm.

"Another day's work and we'll be finished," said the first shearer, busy with a fat sheep. He showed the children how easily he could clip the wool. "Your father hasn't a very big flock. If he had, he wouldn't get *us* to do his shearing!"

"Why not?" asked Rory.

"Well, he'd buy a clipping-machine," said the man. "You should see one at work—it's marvellous! Clips the sheep in no time. And it's better than hand-shearing too, in some ways; a machine can clip a sheep more closely than our hands can, so the fleece weighs more heavily, and brings in more money."

"Perhaps we shall have a clipping-machine next year!" said Rory. "I'd love to work one."

"How much does a fleece weigh?" asked Sheila, looking at the grey fleeces thrown at the back of the shed.

"These fleeces are good," said the shearer. "I reckon they weigh about nine pounds apiece. The shearlings' don't weigh so much of course. That shepherd of yours knows how to look after his sheep. These are fine and healthy!"

The shearers did not stop their work till dusk. Then, tired and thirsty they went to the farm kitchen for food and drink. Harriet made them wash under the pump before they came in.

"You smell like sheep yourselves!" she said. "And my, you're covered with fluff!"

"That was fun!" said Rory, as he and the others went indoors. "Next year we'll get a clipping-machine, and *I* shall work it! My word, I *shall* enjoy that!"

CHAPTER XVI

DOWN TO THE SMITHY

EACH of the children had their own favourite animals or birds on the farm. Sheila, of course, thought the world of her hens, ducklings and chicks. Penny loved her lamb, and all the other little lambs. Benjy and Rory liked the horses best of all.

The farm-horses were enormous. They were Shire horses, large and heavy, slow-moving and tremendously strong. As the children's father had not a great deal of machinery for working his farm, he used his horses a good deal. Benjy and Rory really loved them.

They liked Darling the best, a great dark-brown horse with patient brown eyes and long sweeping eyelashes. Darling was a wonderful worker. She never got tired, and could plod up and down fields for miles from dawn to dusk. All the men on the farm were fond of her, and would bring her a lump of sugar from their tea.

"She's a good horse, that," Bill would say, as he stood leaning over a gate looking at her.

"Ay, she's a fine horse, that," Jim would agree, and the listening children thought so too. Darling's broad back had often carried them home from a distant field, and they loved the regular clip-clop, clip-clop of her big hoofs.

"It's so lovely to wake up in the morning early and hear Darling's big feet clip-clopping along the yard," said Benjy.

"And I love to lie in bed and hear the hens clucking and the ducks quacking," said Sheila.

"And I like to think of Skippetty frisking out there waiting for me," said Penny.

"And I like to hear the cows mooing and the other horses neighing," said Rory. "I say, Benjy—Darling will need shoeing today. Don't you think we could ask Daddy if we could take her down to the smithy? I know the men are going to be busy in the fields."

"Oh, let me go too!" begged Penny. "I do so want to see a horse being shoed. I never have. Does it have to have lots of shoes fitted to see which is the right size?"

"Listen to Penny! Isn't she a baby!" said Rory. "No, silly! Horses have shoes *nailed* on to their hoofs."

"Oh—poor things! Doesn't it hurt them dreadfully?"

said Penny, almost in tears at the thought of nails being driven into a horse's feet. "Oh, I don't think I want to see a horse shoed after all!"

"Well, you'd better," said Rory. "Then you'll see just what happens!"

Daddy said that Rory might take Darling down to be shod. It was Saturday so all the children were free. Of course every one of them wanted to come.

"Well, you can all come—but *I* am going to lead the horse!" said Rory, firmly. He had never taken a horse down to the village smithy before, and it seemed rather a grand thing to do. He didn't want to share it with the others!

"Well, can I ride on Darling's back?" asked Penny.

"Yes, you can do that," said Rory.

They went off to tell Jim that they were to take Darling down to be shoed. Just as they were starting off they saw Tammylan. He had brought some special flower-seeds for their mother. He gave them to Sheila, and said he would come with them to the smithy. Scamper leapt to his shoulder as soon as he saw the wild man, and nibbled gently at his hair.

"Can Skippetty come too?" asked Penny. "I shall be on Darling's back—but Skippetty could go with you, Tammylan."

The lamb was quite willing to follow behind Tammylan. Like all animals it adored him. It skipped round him in delight whenever he came.

Jim led Darling up to Rory. The boy proudly took the horse, and led it out of the gate into the lane.

"You're going to have new shoes!" he said. "Get up. Penny We're going."

Tammylan lifted the little girl up on to the broad back of the horse. "It's like sitting on an enormous sofa!" she said. "Only a sofa doesn't usually go bump-bump-bump like Darling's back!"

They set off down to the village along the lane where

fool's parsley waved its lacy whiteness in every hedgerow. The buttercups were showing in the fields. The distant hills were blue and the countryside was at its very best.

"I wonder what all these flowers are called!" said Sheila, as she bent to pick a bunch from below the hedges. "There is such a lot to learn if you live in the country—the names of flowers and trees and animals and birds—and yet most country folk hardly know any names at all."

"You are right there," said Tammylan. "It is strange that so many people living all their lives in the country know so little about these things! Well, Sheila, make up your mind to know as much as you can! It's fun—as you are so fond of saying!"

Rory was leading Darling on the left-hand side of the lane. Tammylan called to him.

"Rory—take Darling to the right side of the road. A led horse should always be walked on the right."

"Oh goodness, yes—I forgot that," said Rory. "Jim has told me that before."

He took Darling to the right-hand side of the road. The horse was on his left hand, and again Tammylan called to him.

"Go to the other side of the horse, Rory. Take the rope with your right hand, close to its head. Hold the loose end in your left. That's right, old son. Now, if anything startles the horse you have full control of it."

"Thanks, Tammylan," said Rory, who never minded learning anything fresh. "Suppose I was leading a horse and cart—do I keep on the right still?"

"No, left," said Tammylan, "but if you meet a led horse then, you must go to the right. Watch this horse and wagon coming. You are both on the same side of the lane. See what the carter does."

A carter was leading a horse yoked to a farm-wagon. As soon as he saw Rory leading Darling the man took his horse across to the other side of the road, and then back again when he had passed Rory.

"There!" said Tammylan. "That's the rule of the road where horses are concerned, Rory. My goodness me, Skippetty, it's time you learnt the rules of the road too! You nearly ran into the wagon just then!"

They soon came to the smithy. It was an exciting place with a big fire burning at the back. The smith was a great big man with a beard and a brown face. His black curly hair was damp with the heat of the smithy.

"Good morning, young sir," he said to Rory. "So you have brought old Darling for shoes. Ah, she's a fine horse, that one!"

"Everybody says that!" said Penny, slipping down from Darling's broad back. "Are you going to take her old shoes off first, Mr. Smith?"

"Of course!" said the smith, with a laugh. "You watch and see what I do, Missy. Hup, there, Darling, hup you go!"

"Tammylan, why do horses have to wear shoes?" said Penny, slipping her hand into the wild man's big brown one. "Cows don't, do they—or sheep—or cats or dogs."

Tammylan laughed. "Well, Penny," he said, "a horse wouldn't need shoes if he just ran over the soft grass—but he has to walk on our hard roads, and his hoof would break then, if he wore no shoes. His hoof is made of the same kind of stuff as our fingernails, you know—it is a kind of horny case for his foot."

Penny and the others watched the smith. He wore an old leather apron. He lifted Darling's hind foot and looked at it. He took his pincers and pulled away the old shoe from the hoof, and then, with his paring knife, he pared away part of the new-grown hoof.

"What's that raised part in the middle of the horse's hoof?" asked Sheila.

"That is called the frog," said Tammylan. The children laughed.

"What a funny name to give to part of a horse's foot!" said Penny. "Does it croak?"

"Funny joke!" said Rory. "I suppose, Tammylan, that the frog is the bit the horse would walk on if he hadn't a shoe?"

"Yes," said Tammylan. "Now watch the smith make a new shoe for Darling. He is very clever at his job."

All the children watched while the smith took up a straight bar of cold iron. He heated it until it was so hot that it looked white. Then it was easy to bend into the shape of a horse-shoe. The smith hammered it hard. He put it into his fire again and made it hot once more.

"Now he's making the holes for the nails to go through!" said Benjy. "Look at him punching them!"

While the shoe was still hot the smith laid it up against Darling's hoof. "He wants to see if it is pressing evenly all over the hoof," said Tammylan. "No—it isn't quite. Now watch him paring away the bits that the shoe burnt?"

The shoe fitted Darling when the smith once again pressed it against her hoof. The smith put the shoe into cold water and then placed it once more over the hoof. Darling patiently lifted up her foot. She knew exactly what was being done and stood perfectly still.

"He is nailing the shoe to Darling's hoof!" cried Penny. "Oh Tammylan, he's not hurting Darling, is he?"

"Of course not!" said Tammylan. "Does it hurt when your nails are cut, Penny, or when they are filed? Darling doesn't mind a bit! Look—do you see how the nails are bent a little at their points. That is so that they will turn outwards as they are hammered in—otherwise they might go into the fleshy piece of the hoof and hurt Darling. Then she would be lame."

The smith dealt swiftly with the nails in the shoe. Then he rubbed the edges of the hoof well with a rasp—and that was one shoe done! Darling put down her hoof and stamped a little.

"That's to see if it fits!" said Penny. "I stamp in new shoes too!"

The smith took Darling's other hind foot and fitted that with a hot shoe too. "You want to notice that the hind shoes are more pointed than the shoes I'll be making for the forefeet," he said, in his deep voice. "When you pick up a horse-shoe in the road, you'll be able to tell if it's from the fore foot of a horse or the hind foot."

Penny didn't like the smell of burning hoof. She went outside with Skippetty. The others stayed with Tammylan and watched. Benjy wished he could be a smith. He thought it would be a fine life to have a smithy of his own, with a big fire going and all kinds of horses coming in morning, noon and night to be shoed.

"I expect you are very busy, aren't you?" he asked the smith.

"Not one quarter so busy as my father was, and not a tenth so busy as my grandfather!" said the smith. "Ah, in the old days, before motor-cars came along and before farmers got this new machinery to work their farms, there were more horses than we could handle. My trade is all going. There are no carriage horses nowadays, and very few horses on farms! Don't you be a smith, young sir! You'll not make any money at that!"

"Well, I'll see," said Benjy. "One day I may have a farm of my own—then I'll work it with horses and have my own smithy! That would be fine!"

"There—she's finished!" said the smith, giving Darling a smack on her shining back. "Go along, old girl—back to your work!"

Penny mounted on her back again, and the five of them went slowly back up the lane. Tammylan was coming to tea. That was fine. Afterwards they would all go for a walk—and once again the wild man would tell them all he knew about the animals and birds they met.

"When are you coming again?" asked Benjy, when Tammylan said goodbye much later in the day.

"I'll come for the sheep-dipping!" said Tammylan. "I can give a hand there. The sheep do hate it so—and I can quiet them a little. Expect me at the sheep-dipping, Benjy. I think it will have to be done soon!"

CHAPTER XVII

A BAD DAY FOR THE SHEEP

TAMMYLAN was right. Davey had wanted to dip the sheep a week or two back, because he said the flies were getting at them, and laying eggs in the wool. But things kept happening to prevent the dipping, and then Davey found that one or two of the sheep were really in a bad way.

"If we don't dip the sheep as soon as possible, we'll be sorry," he told the children's father.

The children went to look at the dipping-trough. "It looks like a funny kind of bath, sunk into the ground," said Penny. "Isn't it deep—the sheep will have to swim through it, won't they, Rory?"

"Yes, I should think so," said Rory. "It's about eighteen or twenty feet long—goodness, by the time they've swum through that, their wool will be soaked! That's just what we want, of course."

"What's put into the bath?" asked Sheila.

"A very strong disinfectant!" said Rory, proud that he knew so much about it. "The men are going to dip the sheep tomorrow. We'll see all that happens then. How the sheep will hate it, poor things!"

Rory was right! The sheep hated the dipping even more than they hated their shearing. Jim and Bill got the bath ready. They filled it full of water, into which they emptied a big tin of something.

"Pooh, it smells!" said Penny, and she went away a

little. She always hated smells. The men stirred up the bath with sticks. It became cloudy.

Rascal, Tinker and Nancy had got the sheep in from the hills that morning. The flock were in a fold nearby. They bleated, for they knew that something unpleasant was about to happen to them!

"There's Tammylan!" said Rory, pleased. "He said he'd come. Hallo, Tammylan—you're just in time!"

Davey was pleased to see Tammylan. The wild man was so good with animals, and he would be a help in dipping the sheep, who were always very difficult when being dipped in the trough.

"Hallo, children," said Tammylan. "I'm glad your sheep are being dipped today. I reckon it's only just in time to save some of them from illness, Davey."

"How would they be ill?" asked Sheila.

"Well, in this hot weather the flies' eggs hatch out in a few hours in their wool," said Tammylan. "The maggots eat away hungrily and do the sheep a lot of harm. There's a few in your flock that are in a bad way."

"Look!" said Rory. "The first sheep is being driven down the passage-way to the trough!"

Hurdles made a narrow passage from the fold to the swimming-trough. The sheep was made to run down the passage-way and came to the dipping-trough. It stood there, not at all wanting to go in. A farm-hand seized it—and into the bath it went! It bleated piteously as it found itself in the water and struck out with all its legs.

"It's swimming!" cried Penny. "I've never seen a sheep swim before! Look—it's going quite fast!"

The sheep swam through the trough. It seemed a very long way to the panting animal. It was afraid of the water, and afraid of the men who shouted at it. It only wanted to get out and run away!

"Why does the poor sheep have to swim such a long way?" asked Penny indignantly. "It's a shame! Why couldn't they make the bath much shorter?"

"Well, Penny, the disinfectant *must* soak in to every single part of the sheep's wool and skin," said Tammylan. "If the bath were very short, then the sheep might not be thoroughly soaked, and the eggs and maggots might still be alive to work their harm. By making the sheep swim a long way, we make sure that it is soaked to the skin!"

The sheep at last reached the other end of the bath. It went up a slope and stood still in a little enclosed place, shaking itself now and again.

"That place is called the 'dripper'," said Tammylan. "The sheep stand there and let the disinfectant drip off them. See it falling in drops and rivulets off that sheep, Penny? Look how it runs back into the bath, so that very little is wasted!"

The children saw that the disinfectant dripping off the sheep ran back into the trough. They felt sorry for the dripping sheep and hoped that it would soon be allowed to go back to the field.

"Can it soon go back to eat grass on the hills?" asked Penny. "I wish it could."

"Not till it is dry," said Tammylan. "You see, if the liquid drips from the sheep on to the grass, it taints the grass, Penny—and then, if the sheep eat it, they might become ill. So they have to wait a little, and get dry before Davey lets the dogs take them back to the hills to graze."

"Another sheep is going into the dipping-trough!" cried Rory. A second sheep was being driven down—and then a third and a fourth—and soon the air was full of frightened bleatings as the sheep struggled in the water, and swam pantingly to the other end.

The cries of the sheep in the trough made the waiting sheep feel afraid. They ran round the fold and bleated too. Davey looked at Tammylan.

"Can you say a few words to them?" said the old shepherd with a smile.

Tammylan went into the fold. He spoke to the sheep in

The sheep didn't like their bath one little bit!

the deep low voice he kept for animals, and the sheep stood still and listened. It was curious to see Tammylan with animals or birds. They *had* to listen to him. They had to be still. His voice always quieted any animal at once, even if it was in great pain. He had a wonderful way with him.

Benjy watched him. The sheep crowded round the wild man, comforted. They were no longer frightened by the wild bleatings of the sheep being dipped in the trough.

"How I wish I could handle animals as Tammylan does," thought Benjy. "My goodness, if I could, I'd try to tame animals like lions and tigers, bears and elephants! What fun that would be!"

One by one all the sheep had to go down the slope into the trough. They did not make such a fuss now. The men were pleased, because the job was over more quickly when the sheep were docile. It was always a messy job, and they were glad when it was over.

Each sheep stood for a while in the dripper. When half of them were done the water was very dirty indeed. The men emptied it and put in fresh water.

"That's good," said Tammylan, pleased. "That gives the rest of the sheep a good chance to be thoroughly disinfected now. It's a mistake to use the water too much before changing it."

As soon as the sheep left the dripper they went into a big fold and there they had to stay until they were dry and there was no fear of drippings spoiling their grass.

Rascal, Tinker and Nancy lay down, patiently waiting until the sheep were ready. Then they would take them off to the hills again, at a wave of the hand from old Davey. They kept well away from the trough! They had no wish to be bathed there too!

Penny suddenly missed Skippetty. Where could he be? Had he been frightened by the bleatings and gone running away by himself somewhere? The little girl called him.

"Skippetty! Skippetty! Where are you? Come here, Skippetty!"

A pitiful bleating answered her—and to Penny's horror she saw Skippetty running down into the dipping-trough with some other sheep! He had got into the fold and had to take his turn.

"Oh, stop Skippetty, stop him!" cried Penny. "Oh, he'll be drowned! Davey, save him!"

But it was too late to stop the lamb from going into the trough. In he went with the others, and scrambled through, bleating at the top of his loud voice. He climbed out, with everyone laughing at him.

Penny rushed to get him. "No, Tuppenny, no!" cried Davey. "Don't you touch him while he's fresh from the bath. You'll get yourself all messed. Let him stand in the dripper with the others. That lamb of yours is always up to something!"

So poor Skippetty had to stand in the dripper with the others, and then he went into the fold to dry. Penny was dreadfully upset, but the others laughed loudly.

"You *are* horrid to laugh at poor Skippetty!" said Penny, almost in tears. "What would you feel like if your squirrel went into that horrid dipping-trough, Benjy?"

"Oh, he wouldn't be so silly," said Benjy, putting his hand up to caress Scamper, who, as usual, was on his shoulder. "You must teach Skippetty a little common sense, Penny—though you could do with some yourself sometimes!"

Penny said that Skippetty smelt, after he had dried himself. She was torn in two—for she wanted to pet the lamb and comfort him after his horrid bath—and yet she could not bear to have her hands smell horrid. So she went and put on her old gloves, which made everyone laugh still more loudly!

"Don't you worry, Tuppenny!" cried Davey. "Your lamb hasn't come to any harm. It has probably done him good. You watch and see how much better my sheep are, after their bath!"

So they were. They were much livelier and happier, and Davey was pleased with them. "You see, all the eggs and grubs are gone now," he said. "If I can keep my sheep healthy and fit, the flies are not so likely to go to them, and I shan't have to keep dipping them. One year I had to dip sheep so many times that they almost got used to it!"

"Was there ever a year when you didn't dip them at all?" asked Penny.

"Well, there's a law that says we *must* dip our sheep so many times each year," said Davey. "It's a good law. It stops disease from spreading among the flocks. One careless farmer can do a lot of harm to others, you know. We should take as much care of our animals as we do of ourselves."

"I never knew there were so many things to be done on a farm," said Rory, seriously. "As I mean to be a farmer when I grow up I'm glad I'm learning now. Farming's fine, isn't it, Davey?"

"It's a man's job!" said Davey. "Ay, young sir, it's a man's job!"

CHAPTER XVIII

EVERYBODY HAS A JOB!

THE weeks went happily by. The children went off to their lessons on week-days, and enjoyed their Saturdays and Sundays immensely. There was always something fresh to do on the farm. The weather was fine and sunny, and the children became as brown as acorns.

The dairy was doing well. Mother was delighted, because her cream and butter sold well. Everybody praised the butter and said how delicious it was. Harriet was very deft in the way she put it up into half-pound and pound pats, and Sheila had learnt to wrap them up very neatly.

Sheila felt happy those summer days, as she worked in the cool dairy with her mother and Harriet. It was such fun to separate the cream from the milk, and to churn the butter from the cream. It was lovely to be allowed to pat and squeeze the butter till it was just right to be cut up and wrapped. Sheila felt proud when she saw the neat piles of yellow butter sitting on the dairy shelves, wrapped in "WILLOW FARM" paper.

She and Fanny had been very good indeed with the hens. They had set two more clutches of eggs under two broody hens, and had brought off twenty-four chicks, much to their pride and delight. Now the farmyard was full of hens, half-grown pullets and chicks—to say nothing of the fine batch of ducks that swam gaily on the pond from dawn to dusk.

The two girls had sold a great many eggs, and had made quite a lot of money. They still kept their egg-book most carefully, and Sheila felt quite grown-up when she showed her parents all that was in it.

The piglets had grown marvellously too, and were big and fat and round. They rooted about in the orchard all day long. The sow was a contented old thing, and the children couldn't help liking her, though she was no beauty.

Rory and Benjy had been taught how to groom the horses. Their father said that it would be a help in the busy summertime, if the boys could sometime groom the horses for Jim in the mornings. Then Jim could get on with something else.

Of course Rory and Benjy were simply delighted, for they both adored the big Shire horses. Captain, Blossom and Darling were their favourites.

Jim showed the boys how to groom them. "You stand

on the near side of the horse first," he said. "The near side is the left side, of course. Now take the brush in your left hand and the curry-comb in your right. That's the way Rory."

"What a funny comb!" said Penny, who was watching in great interest. "I shouldn't like to comb *my* hair with that."

"It's got iron teeth," said Rory. "What do I do next, Jim?"

"Begin at the head, Rory," said Jim. "Comb and brush in turn. Now the neck—then the shoulder—the fore-leg. Go on—that's right. Work vigorously—the horse likes it."

Rory combed and brushed hard. It made him hot, but he didn't mind. It was lovely to work with horses like this. It was a real job, Rory thought.

"Knock your comb hard against the stall to get out the dirt and hair," said Jim. So Rory tapped the comb to clean it. The others watched him, wishing they could curry-comb a horse too. Benjy meant to have his turn the next day!

"When you've finished this side of the horse, get on with the other side," said Jim. "I'll leave you to it now. Feed Darling when you've finished her—then I'll come back and help you to harness her."

In a week or two both Rory and Benjy could manage the horses beautifully. They were really almost as good as the men, and their father was proud of them. Benjy was really better than Rory because he was very good with all animals, and they loved him to handle them.

Penny was always interested to see the bit being put into a horse's mouth. "How does it go in so nicely?" she asked. "It seems to fit beautifully."

Jim opened Darling's mouth and showed the little girl the horse's strong teeth. "Look," he said, "there is a space between Darling's front and back teeth—just there, see—and that is where the bit goes, quite comfortably."

"Oh," said Penny, looking sad, "did you pull out those teeth to make room for the bit, Jim? How unkind!"

Jim laughed loudly. Penny always said such funny things.

"No, no," he said, "we don't do things like that! A horse always has that space—teeth never grow there—so we just put in the bit in that space and the horse is quite comfortable."

"Oh," said Penny, "I'm glad you don't have to pull teeth out to make room for it. Isn't it a good thing that the horse's teeth are made like that?"

One of the things that made Penny very happy that summer was the coming of the three calves. They were born on the farm. The cows who had the calves were called Buttercup, Clover and Daisy, and were lovely red and white creatures, with soft brown eyes.

The calves were like their mothers, and were really adorable. Penny went to see them twenty times a day at the very least. They sucked at her little hand, and she liked that. They were playful little things, not a bit staid like the big fat cows.

"Daddy, I want to look after the calves," said Penny seriously, when she heard that the calves were born. "I really do. Sheila and Fanny manage the hens by themselves now—they don't want me to help at all. Rory and Benjy are doing the horses. I've only got Skippetty to see to, and now that he eats the grass, I don't even have to feed him out of the bottle."

"But Penny dear, you're too little to be of any *real* help!" said her father, who still thought of Penny as a very small girl. "You're only eight."

"Well, I can't help that," said Penny, almost crying. "I want to be nine as soon as possible, but a year takes such a long time to go. I do think you might let me have the calves, Daddy. Tammylan said he felt sure I could manage them well. He says they are awfully easy, if they are healthy from the beginning—and ours are."

In the end Penny got her way, though Harriet was to help her at first. The little girl was overjoyed.

"Ah, Skippetty, I shall be doing real work now, like the others!" she said to her lamb, who, as usual, followed her everywhere. "You'll be quite jealous when you see me feeding the calves, Skippetty—but I shan't feed them out of a bottle as I did you!"

Harriet put milk in pails for the three calves. They were out in the fields all day long, but at night they were brought back to the sheds. Penny went with Harriet to feed the calves.

"Now you look what I do," said Harriet, setting down the pails in front of the calves. "They don't know how to drink yet, bless them—they're so new-born! Well, we have to teach them. They know how to suck, as all little creatures do—but these calves have to learn drinking, not sucking. We must teach them."

"How?" asked Penny. "Skippetty sucked out of a bottle—but the calves can't do that, they're too big."

"Now watch me," said Harriet. She dipped her fingers into a pail of milk till they were dripping with the white liquid. She held out her hand to the nearest calf. It took no notice. Harriet put her milky fingers against its mouth. The calf at once smelt the milk and opened its mouth. In half a second it was sucking Harriet's hand.

"Oh but Harriet, it will take ages and ages to feed the calves that way!" said Penny, looking with dismay at the big pails of milk.

Harriet laughed. "Watch, Penny, watch," she said. She drew her hand slowly away towards the pail of milk. The calf, eager to suck her hand, followed it down with its mouth. Harriet quickly dipped her hand in the milk again and held it out to the calf. Then, as it sucked hard, she drew her hand away once more, and put it slowly into the milk. The calf followed her hand hungrily—and put its nose right into the pail!

It sucked at Harriet's fingers busily, and as its mouth

was now in the milk, it sucked and drank at the same time!

"Oh, that's clever of you, Harriet!" said Penny. "Take your hand away and see if the calf will drink by itself."

But it wouldn't. It wanted Harriet's fingers to suck, even though it could drink the milk as well! So Harriet kept her hand in the milk, and the calf sucked and drank hungrily.

"Please let me do that for the second calf," begged Penny. "I know I can."

So Harriet let her, and to Penny's enormous delight, the little creature sucked at her small hand and followed it greedily down to the milk, just as the first calf had done with Harriet.

"Good," said Harriet. "Well, Penny, that's the first step! It won't be long before the calves come running at the smallest clink of a pail!"

Harriet was quite right. The calves soon learnt to drink the milk, and when Penny carried out the pails one by one, she had to be careful that the hungry calves did not knock them over!

She had to feed them three times a day—before breakfast, at midday, and before she went to bed. It was lovely work and the little girl enjoyed it. It made her feel important and grown-up to have something of her very own to manage.

For nine weeks Penny fed the calves three times a day. They were given the separated milk, which had no cream, and Harriet taught Penny to put a few drops of cod-liver-oil into the pails, to make up for the lack of cream. The little girl always measured it out very carefully, and never once forgot.

The piglets had the buttermilk and loved it. Penny was glad that her calves had better milk than the pigs! When they were just over two months old she only had to feed them morning and night. Then very soon they would be put on to solid food—hay, turnips, things like that.

Penny asked all kinds of questions and was sure she could manage the calves even when they grew older.

The calves grew well. They loved Penny, and as soon as she appeared at the gate of their field with Skippetty, they ran to her, flinging their long tails into the air. Whether she brought them food or not, they were always pleased to see her.

At night she fetched them from the field and put them into a big well-aired shed. She saw that they had plenty of clean straw, and looked after them so well that the other children were quite astonished.

"Penny, you're growing up!" said Rory, solemnly. "You really are!"

"Oh, am I!" said Penny, delighted. "How lovely! I always seem so small to myself, when I'm with you others. But I really feel big and important when I'm managing the calves. So perhaps I really am growing up now!"

"Don't grow up too fast, little Penny!" said Tammylan, who was watching her take the calves to their field. "Calves are nicer than cows—lambs are sweeter than sheep—chicks are prettier than hens— and children are nicer than grown-ups! So don't grow up *just* yet!"

"Oh, I won't," said Penny, slipping her hand into the wild man's. "Not really for years and years. But I do like to *feel* grown-up even if I'm not, Tammylan."

"Well, you're doing your bit on the farm," said Tammylan. "You all are. You're children to be proud of. I really don't know what the farm would do without you now!"

CHAPTER XIX

A VISIT TO TAMMYLAN—AND A STORM

In June the hay-fields at Willow Farm were a lovely sight. The grass waved in them, and all kinds of flowers peeped here and there. The children loved to walk beside the hedges that ran round the fields. They were not allowed to wander in the grass, of course, for fear of spoiling the hay—and Skippetty had to be kept out too.

"The hay crop is good this year," said the children's father, pleased. "That means that we shall have plenty of hay for the cattle in the winter—good feeding for them. Well—when hay-making time comes I am going to get you four children a holiday, because we shall want your help!"

"Oh good!" cried everyone, delighted at the idea of an unexpected holiday.

"We'll work jolly hard," said Rory. "Feel the muscles in my arm, Daddy—aren't they getting hard?"

His father felt them. "My word, they are!" he said, surprised. He looked at Rory closely. "Who would have thought you were the same boy as the ill-grown, pale, weedy Rory of last year!" he said. "Well, we work hard—but it's worth it when I look at you all, and see how bonny and rosy you are. Now about this hay-making—we shall begin on Monday, because the weather is beautiful at present."

"Can we only make hay properly when the weather is nice, then?" asked Penny.

"Well, you surely know the old saying 'Make hay while the sun shines!'" said her father. "Yes—we have to cut and cart the hay while the weather is dry and warm. Wet hay isn't much good, and needs a lot more labour."

"It has to be cut, and turned, carted away and stacked, hasn't it?" said Rory, remembering what had happened at Cherry Tree Farm the year before. "Daddy, what happens if hay is stacked before it is quite dry?"

"It becomes very hot," said his father. "So hot that the hay actually gets blackened by the heat—and it may even get on fire. I remember one summer helping your Uncle Tim with his hay, and it was such wet weather that it was impossible to get it really dry."

"What did you do, then?" asked Rory.

"We had to put thick layers of straw into the hay-stack as we built it," said his father. "That prevented the hay from becoming too hot because the straw sucked up the moisture. The straw made splendid fodder for the winter, I remember."

"I do like hearing all these things," said Rory. "I shall remember them when I have a farm of my own."

The children went to find Tammylan on Sunday, to tell him that hay-making would begin the next day. Tammylan was not in his cave, so they guessed that he must be in his tree-house by the river. They went to see.

Tammylan's tree-house was a lovely place. It was built of willows which, although cut from the trees, still grew green leaves—so that it looked almost as if Tammylan lived in a growing house! The children loved it. The wild man had a bed of heather and bracken. It was there in the house, but Tammylan was nowhere to be seen.

"I wonder where he is," said Benjy, looking all round. "Oh look—there's the hare! It's come to the tree-house with Tammylan!"

The hare was crouching in a corner, half-afraid of the children. But when Benjy went towards it, it did not run away. It knew he was a friend, and heard in the boy's voice the same gentle, friendly tones that it knew in Tammylan's. It allowed Benjy to stroke it, and then, with a few swift bounds it fled out of the tree-house into the woods.

"It does limp a bit," said Benjy, watching. "But it's wonderful the way its poor legs mended. How can we find Tammylan, I wonder?"

"Send Scamper to look for him!" said Penny.

"Good idea!" said Benjy. "Where *is* Scamper?"

The squirrel was bounding about the tree-house, sniffing for his friend, Tammylan. Benjy spoke to him. "Scamper—find Tammylan, find him!"

Scamper was very sharp. He understood what Benjy meant, because he himself wanted to find the wild man too! So off he went into the tree, keeping a sharp look-out for Tammylan from the branches.

And before very long the four children saw their friend coming from the river-bank with Scamper on his shoulder!

"Hallo, Tammylan!" they shouted. "So Scamper found you!"

"Yes, he made me jump!" said the wild man. "I was lying down on the banks, watching a kingfisher catching fish, when suddenly this rascal landed right in the middle of my back! I knew that you must be somewhere about so I came to see."

The children went with the wild man to watch the brilliant kingfisher fishing. It was marvellous to see how he sat on a low branch, watching for fish in the water below.

"There he goes!" cried Penny, as the blue and green bird flashed down to the water. He was back again in a second, with a small fish in his mouth. He banged it against the bough and killed it. Then he flew off with it.

"Isn't he going to eat it?" asked Penny.

"He would have liked to!" said Tammylan. "But he has a nest at the end of a tunnel in a bank nearby—and no doubt his wife is sitting on a nest of fish-bones, warming her white eggs, hoping that her mate will soon bring her something to eat. Well—she will have fish for dinner!"

"Tammylan, we came to tell you something," said

Benjy, lying on his back and looking up into the brilliant blue sky. "I say—isn't it gorgeous weather!"

"Is that what you came to tell me?" asked Tammylan, looking astonished.

"No, of course not!" said Benjy, laughing. "We came to tell you that we are having a holiday for a few days—so will you come and see us?"

"But why the holiday?" asked Tammylan. "Have you been specially good at your lessons lately? I can't believe it!"

The children laughed. "No," said Rory, "but we are going to begin hay-making tomorrow. Won't that be fun, Tammylan?"

But Tammylan did not smile. He looked worried.

"What's the matter, Tammylan?" asked Penny.

"I hope you *won't* begin hay-making tomorrow," said Tammylan. "There will be a great thunderstorm tomorrow night—with a good deal of rain. It would be best to put off your hay-making until the end of the week, although I know that the hay is ready now."

"Tammylan! How can you possibly know that a thunderstorm is coming?" said Benjy, sitting up. "Why, it feels simply lovely today—not a bit thundery."

"To you, perhaps," said Tammylan, "but you must remember that I live out of doors all the time, and I know the weather as well as you know your tables! You can't live as I do, looking at the sky and the hills day and night, feeling the wind on my cheek, seeing how the trees blow, without knowing exactly what the weather is going to be. And I am quite sure that there will be a storm tomorrow night, and your hay will be spoilt if it is cut tomorrow. The weather will clear again on Tuesday, the wind will be fresh, the days warm, and the hay will be perfect for cutting by Thursday or Friday."

"We must tell Daddy," said Rory, at once. "Oh Tammylan, I hope he believes what you say! Bother! We shan't have a holiday tomorrow!"

"Well, that doesn't matter, surely, if you save your hay-crop, does it?" said Tammylan.

"Of course not," said Rory. "Well, we'd better get back and tell Daddy at once, or he will be making all kinds of arrangements for the hay-making."

The children said goodbye and went quickly home. They ran to find their father. He was in the fields, looking at the cattle. They ran to him.

"Daddy! Don't cut the hay tomorrow! There will be a storm and heaps of rain tomorrow night!" cried Benjy. "Tammylan says so."

"Oh, Tammylan says so, does he?" said his father, looking thoughtful. "Well, well—I don't know what to do. I've made all arrangements to start tomorrow—but Tammylan has a strange way of foretelling the weather. Look, there's old Davey the shepherd. Call him here and we'll see if he thinks there will be a storm too."

The children yelled to Davey. He came up with Tinker close at his heels. The other dogs were guarding the sheep.

"Davey, what do you think about the hay-making to-morrow?" asked the children's father.

"The grass is in fine fettle," said the old shepherd. "And the weather's right. But I doubt you'll get caught by a storm tomorrow."

"That's just what Tammylan said!" cried Penny.

Davey's grey eyes twinkled at her. "Did he, Tuppenny?" he said. "Well now, that's not surprising, seeing that he and I spend our days watching the things that make the weather! The clouds tell us many things, the way the trees turn in the wind, the feel of the air, the look of the far-away hills. And I say there's thunder coming, and a mighty storm. So, sir, if I were you, I'd put off the hay-making tomorrow, and wait for a day or two till the rain's dried out, and you can cut in safety. 'Twould be a pity to spoil a fine crop like yours!"

"Thanks, Davey," said the farmer, and the old shepherd

went on his way, his dog at his heels. The four children looked at their father.

"Well, hay-making is off," he said. "We'll see if the storm comes. If it does, we'll be glad the hay wasn't cut—if it doesn't, there's no harm done. We can cut the next day!"

So the children went to school after all on Monday. They looked up at the sky. It was brilliant blue, without a single cloud to be seen.

"Perfect for cutting hay," said Rory. "Oh goodness—I wonder if that storm will come tonight."

When the children went to bed that night the sky was still clear. But Mother said she had a thunder-headache, and Harriet said that some of the milk had gone sour.

"There's a storm coming," she said. And sure enough there was! The children awoke at two o'clock in the morning to the sound of an enormous crash of thunder! They lay open-eyed in their beds. Then the lightning flashed vividly and lighted up the room. The children leapt out of bed and ran to their windows. They all loved a good thunderstorm.

The wind blew through the trees with a curious swishing noise. Then the rain came down. It fell first in a few big drops, and then it pelted down savagely, slashing at the trees and the flowers, the corn and the grass as if it wanted to lay them to the ground.

Crash after crash of thunder came and rolled around the sky. The lightning lit up the whole of the countryside and the children were quite silent, marvelling at the magnificent sight. Fanny crept into their room, trembling.

"Oh please, Miss Sheila, can I come in here with you?" she asked, in a quivering voice. "I can't wake Aunt Harriet, and I'm so frightened."

"*Frightened!*" said Sheila and Penny together, in astonishment. "What are you frightened of?"

"The storm!" said poor Fanny.

"But why?" asked Penny. "It won't hurt you! It's grand and beautiful. Come and watch it!"

"Oh no, thank you," said Fanny, crouching behind the wardrobe. "I can't think how you dare to stand at the window."

"Have you ever been hurt by a storm?" asked Sheila. "You haven't? Well, then, why are you frightened, Fanny?"

"Oh, my mother always used to hide under a bed when there was a storm," said Fanny. "And that used to frighten me terribly. So I always knew there was something dreadful about a storm!"

"How funny you are!" said Sheila, going to Fanny. "You're not frightened of the storm itself—but only because your mother showed you *she* was frightened. Don't be silly! Come and watch."

So Fanny went to watch—and when she saw how marvellous the countryside looked when it was lit up so vividly by the lightning, she forgot her fear and marvelled at it just as the others did.

"My word, it's a good thing we didn't cut the hay today!" she said. "That would have been out in the field, lying cut—and the rain would have soaked it so much that we'd have had to turn it time and time again! Now if we get sunny weather and a fresh wind tomorrow, it will dry standing and be quite all right in a day or two."

"Tammylan was quite right," said Rory. "He always is! I *am* glad we took his advice. Good old Tammylan!"

CHAPTER XX

MAKING HAY WHILE THE SUN SHINES

THE weather cleared up again on Tuesday, and the sky shone brilliant blue.

"I can't see a single cloud," said Sheila to Fanny, when she went to feed the hens. "Not one! But look at the puddles everywhere underfoot! We must have had torrents of rain last night."

"We did," said Fanny. "The duck-pond is almost overflowing this morning—and the ducks are as pleased as can be to find puddles everywhere. Wouldn't it be nice to have webbed feet and to go splashing through every puddle we came to!"

Sheila laughed. "That's the sort of thing Penny would say!" she said. "Look—there she is, taking the calves to their field. Penny! Penny! Isn't everywhere wet this morning?"

"Yes," shouted back Penny. "The grass is soaking my shoes. They're as wet as can be. What a good thing we didn't cut the hay yesterday—it would be terribly wet today."

By the end of the day the hot sun had dried the grass well. A fresh wind sprang up that night and finished the drying, so that the children's father felt sure that it would be safe to cut the hay on Thursday.

"We've got a holiday till Monday!" cried Rory, joyfully, when he heard the news. "Isn't that marvellous! Daddy says we've to be up at dawn tomorrow to start the hay-making. Everyone's going to help this week, even Mother and Harriet."

Darling and Blossom dragged along the machine that

cut the grass. It fell in swathes behind them, and soon the hay-fields looked as shaven and shorn as the sheep had looked after their shearing. In a very short while the cut hay turned to a grey-green colour, and a sweet smell rose on the air.

"I love the smell of the hay!" said Sheila, sniffing it. "No wonder the cattle like to have it to eat in the winter. I feel as if I wouldn't mind it myself!"

The new-mown hay did smell lovely, especially in the evening. It was so beautifully dry that the farmer said it need only be turned once.

The hay lay in long rows. The children played about in it to their heart's content, flinging handfuls at one another, and burying themselves under the delicious-smelling hay.

"It doesn't matter us messing about in the hay-fields like this, does it?" said Penny.

"Not a bit," said her father. "The more the hay is flung about the better I shall like it! You are helping to dry it. Tomorrow it must be properly turned."

"How was hay cut before machines were invented?" asked Rory. "Was it cut by hand?"

"Yes," said his father. "And a long job it must have been too! The big hay-fields were all cut down by men using scythes—sharp curved blades, set in a large handle—and it took them days to mow it. Our modern machines help us a great deal. I wish I had more of them—but when the farm begins to pay I shall buy what I can, and you shall learn how to use the machines on Willow Farm."

"Good," said Rory, pleased.

The next day everyone worked hard in the hay-fields, turning the hay over with hand-rakes, so that the moist bits underneath could be exposed to the sun and well-dried. The hay was in fine condition and the farmer was pleased. He looked up at the sky.

"This hot dry weather is just right for the hay," he said. "I'm glad we took Tammylan's advice and waited a few days."

Tammylan was helping to make hay too. He and the children had great fun together, especially when they found Penny and Skippetty fast asleep in a corner, and buried them both very carefully under a pile of the sweet-smelling hay. Penny couldn't *think* where she was when she awoke, and found the hay all on top of her!

"We must get the hay into windrows," said the farmer. "Big long rows all down the field."

"Oh," said Sheila, in dismay. "What a lot of hard work that will mean!"

"Not for you!" said her father. "We will let Captain do that work for us! He will pull the horse-rake that rakes the hay into windrows."

Rory helped Jim to get out the big horse-rake. It was twelve or fourteen feet wide, and had two strong wheels and a number of hinged steel teeth. Captain was harnessed to it and was soon set to work. The big horse was guided up and down the hayfields by Rory.

Penny went to watch, running along beside the machine. "Rory, it's clever!" she cried. "The big steel teeth slide along under the hay and collect it all."

"Yes," said Rory, proudly. "Now watch what happens. The rake is full of hay—so I pull this handle—and that lifts up the row of steel teeth—and the big load of hay is dropped in a long row on the field. That's cleverer still, isn't it, Penny?"

The horse-rake did the work of six or seven men. Jim and Rory worked it by turns, and soon the hay-fields were beautiful with long windrows of turned hay.

The next thing was to build it up into hay-cocks—small stacks of hay down the field. The children helped with this, and when they left the field one evening, tired out but happy, they thought that the hay-cocks looked simply lovely, standing so peacefully in the fields as if they were dreaming about the sun and wind and rain had had helped them to grow when they were grass.

"What else has to be done to the hay?" asked Penny.

Darling stood patiently as the children helped unload her

"It's got to be built into hay-stacks," said Tammylan, picking up the tired little girl and carrying her on his shoulder. "You'll find that Bill is the best man at that! He knows how to thatch, and can build the best hay-stack for miles around."

"I shouldn't have thought that it was very difficult to build a hay-stack," said Penny, sleepily. "Just piling the hay higher and higher."

Tammylan laughed at her. "You wait till you see one being built," he said. "Then you won't think it is quite such an easy job!"

The hay was carted to the rick-yard on the old hay-wagon. The children liked that. They climbed on the top of every wagon-load and rode there, while Darling went clip-clop, clip-clop down the lanes that smelt of honey-suckle. The hedges reached out greedy fingers and clutched at the hay as it passed.

"You can see the way we go by the bits of hay on the hedges!" said Sheila. "Oh, isn't it fun to lie here on the top of the hay-wagon, with the soft hay under us, and the blue summer sky above. I hope Darling doesn't mind our extra weight!"

Darling certainly didn't. It made no difference at all to her whether she had four, six or twelve children on the hay-wagon. She plodded down the lanes to the rick-yard, strong, slow and patient.

Some of the hay was stored in a shed, but the farmer hadn't enough room for it all, so most of it was to be built into stacks. Bill took command at once.

The field stack was begun. The children watched with great interest. It was a big stack, and was to be oblong. When it was fairly high, Bill and two other men stood up on the top.

"We've got to press the hay down as much as we can," he told the children. "Ah, here comes another wagon-load."

The hay-wagon was pulled up close to the stack. Rory

was allowed to climb up on top of the hay and use a pitch-fork. He had to toss the hay from the wagon to where Bill stood waiting for it on the half-built stack.

"You watch your pitch-fork well, the first few times you use it," Jim warned Rory. "It's a dangerous thing till you're well used to it."

Rory was very careful indeed. He turned away from the man helping him, so that his fork would not jab him at all, and threw the hay quite cleverly from the wagon to the stack. The men there worked hard and well, tramping down the hay and stacking it firmly and neatly. The stack rose higher and higher.

Benjy was told to go round the stack with a rake. "Rake out the loose bits of hay," said Jim. "You can keep the stack for us and make the sides neat. Is your father down there? Good. He'll tell us if the stack gets a bit lop-sided and will prop it up till we put it right."

"I'll get an elevator next year if I can," said the farmer. "That sends the hay up by machinery and saves a lot of labour."

Rory thought that an elevator would be a very good thing, for he was tired out by the time that the stack was finished! His arms ached with throwing the hay!

Bill thatched the stack beautifully to keep the rain out. He had made the centre of the top of the thatch higher than the surrounding sides, so that the rain could run down and drop off the eaves, just as it runs down the roof of a house.

"And now to give the finishing touch!" said the thatcher. The children watched him. He twisted up some hay together and began to make something at the very top of the stack in the middle. The children saw that it was a crown!

"There!" said Bill. "Now anyone coming this way will know that I've built and thatched this stack, for the crown at the top is my mark."

"It does look fine," said Penny, admiringly. "It's such

a big fat stack, and smells so nice. How the animals will love to eat the hay from it, when it is cut in the winter from the big stack!"

Hay-making time was over when the last stack was built and finished. Three fine stacks then stood in the rick-yard and the farmer and his men were pleased. They liked to think that there was such good fodder for their animals in the winter. The children liked the stacks too, and often remembered the waving grass, so beautiful in the wind, that had gone to make the sturdy stacks on the farm.

"I'm sorry hay-making time is over," said Penny. "That's really been most exciting. I'm sure there won't be anything *quite* so exciting on Willow Farm this year."

"Wait till harvest-time!" said Rory. "That's the big event of the year! You wait till then, Penny!"

CHAPTER XXI

HARVEST HOME

THE summer was very fine and warm that year. The four children grew browner and browner, and Penny grew so plump that Rory said he was sure he would one day mistake her for one of the fat piglets!

Everything grew, just as the children did! The wheat and the clover were strong and sturdy, the potato fields were a sight to see, and the other crops looked healthy and well-grown.

"Well, it may be beginner's luck," said Uncle Tim, one day when he came over, "but your farm is certainly flourishing this year! It's doing a good deal better than mine. I've got four cows ill of some mysterious disease, and my wheat is very poor."

"Well, the children have been a great help to me, bless them," said the farmer. "Sheila really manages wonderfully with the poultry, and helps in the dairy too, and little Penny has looked after the calves just as well as Jim or Bill might have. As for my two boys, I don't know what I should do without them—they see to the horses for me, and work as hard in the fields as anyone."

"Well, you'll need all the help you can get at harvest-time," said Uncle Tim. "You've a fine grain crop, no doubt about that! My word, you'll make some money this year—and be able to buy all the machinery I've been longing for myself for years! Lucky man!"

When the summer was full, the farmer went to look at his wheat fields with the children. They looked lovely.

"The corn is such a beautiful golden colour!" said Sheila, "and I do love to see it bend and make waves of itself when the wind blows."

"I like the whispering noise it makes," said Penny. "It always seems to me as if every stalk of wheat is whispering a secret to the next one—and the next one is listening with its ear!"

Everybody laughed. "An ear of corn can't hear, silly!" said Rory.

"Well, the ears always bend to one another as if they *are* listening," said Penny, going red.

"It's a lovely idea of yours, little Penny," said her father.

"First the corn was like a green mist over the brown field," said Sheila. "Then it grew thicker and greener and taller. Then it was tall enough to wave itself about, and looked rather like the sea. Then it grew taller still and turned this lovely golden colour. Is it ripe yet, Daddy?"

"Yes," said her father, picking an ear of corn and rubbing it between his hands. "Beautifully ripe. Just ready for reaping."

"How are we going to reap it?" asked Rory. "With

sickles or scythes? I've always wanted to use one—swish, swish, swish—and down goes the corn!"

"I've no doubt that that is the way the corn in this field was cut many years ago," said his father. "And it still is cut that way on some very small farms. But not on this one! I'm going to borrow your uncle's reaping-machine. It's a very old-fashioned one but it will reap our fields all right! Then next year maybe I can buy a really modern machine—one called a tractor-binder—a really marvellous machine."

"When are you going to begin the reaping?" asked Penny, eagerly. "We've got our summer holidays now and we can help."

"We'll begin it this week," said her father. "I'll telephone to Uncle Tim tonight and see if he can lend us his machine. He won't be reaping just yet because his crops are rather later than ours this year."

The next excitement was the arrival of the reaping-machine. It came clanking up the lane to Willow Farm drawn by two horses. They were Boy and Beauty, two of Uncle Tim's strongest horses. Rory unharnessed them, and the carter who had come with the machine led back the two horses to Cherry Tree Farm.

The children looked at the reaping-machine. Jim explained it to them. "See this long bar that rides a few inches from the ground?" he said. "That's the cutter bar. Look at its steel fingers. And now see this bar—it's the knife bar—look at the sharp knives it is fitted with. Now when the reaper goes along the knives pass between the teeth of the cutter bar—and the corn is cut just as if big scissors were snipping it down!"

"Oh, isn't that clever!" said Rory. "What happens to the corn when it is cut like that?" Does it fall to the ground?"

"It falls on to this little platform," said Jim. "It has to be raked off by hand by the man who sits on the seat here. Then the cut corn is gathered up by the people following behind—we call them lifters, because they lift up the corn—and they bind it into sheaves."

"I'm longing to see the reaper at work," said Benjy. "Is it starting today, Jim?"

"Right now," said Jim. "I'm just going to get Darling and Blossom to pull it. You get them for me, Rory, will you, then I can have a word with your father about which field he wants reaping first."

Rory and Benjy went proudly off to get the two big horses, who were in the nearby field, waiting to be set to work. The boys led them back to the reaper and harnessed the patient animals to it.

The reaper was taken to the glowing field of yellow corn. The children gathered round, watching. Bill took the reins to guide the horses. Jim sat on the reaping-machine with a wooden rake. The machine was started, and the two horses pulled with all their might.

How the corn fell! It was cut as neatly and as quickly as if somebody with an enormous pair of scissors had snipped off great patches of it! Jim pushed off the cut corn as it fell on the little platform or tilting-board as he called it, and it tumbled to the ground.

Behind the reaper worked the other men of the farm—and Mother, Harriet and Fanny as well! Yes, everyone had to help at harvest-time, and how they loved it, although it was not easy. But it was so lovely out there in the golden sunshine, working together, laughing and chattering in the corn.

The children watched to see what the "lifters" did. They gathered up a bundle of the cut corn, and tied each one round with wisps of straw.

"I've made a sheaf!" said Penny, suddenly. The others looked. Sure enough, the little girl had managed to tie up a bundle of corn very neatly with some stalks, and there was her sheaf—a bit smaller than the sheaves that the others lifters had made, it was true—but still, a very neat and presentable one!

"You others can try your hands at making the sheaves!" called Mother. "It's just a knack. The more we do, the better for the corn. Once it is in sheaves, we can stand it up in shocks."

So all the children tried their hand at being lifters too. Very soon they had become quite good at gathering and binding the corn into sheaves—though Penny was rather slower than the others. Soon they had made enough sheaves to build up into a nice shock.

"Sixteen sheaves to a shock!" called out Jim, as he went by with the reaper. "Set up the sheaves in pairs—lean them against one another—that's right, Rory. See how many shocks you children can make!"

Penny got tired of gathering up the corn and binding it, so the others let her stand up the sheaves and make shocks for them. She liked doing that. "Don't the shocks look fine?" she said, as she finished a very neat one. "This is as good as building castles on the sea-shore!"

The reaping and binding went on all day long. The farmer was pleased with the way the work went.

"Next year, when I buy a self-binder," he said, "you will not have nearly so much work to do!"

"Why?" asked Sheila. "Does it do even more work than our reaper does?"

"Oh yes!" said her father. "It not only cuts the corn, but it gathers it into sheaves, ties each one neatly round with strong string, and then throws each sheaf out on to the ground! It's like magic! It goes through the field of waving corn leaving rows of sheaves behind it. So all you will have to do next year is to pick up the sheaves and place them in shocks, ready to be carted away!"

When all the corn-fields were reaped, and lay quiet and still with rows of shocks in the evening sun, everyone was glad.

Tammylan came down to see the fields and nodded his head as he saw the fine shocks. "It's a good crop," he said to the farmer. "You've had luck this year. It won't be long before you can cart the corn to the rick-yard, for it's already as dry as can be."

The wild man slipped his brown hand into the middle of a nearby sheaf. He felt about and then withdrew his hand. "The corn's in rattling order!" he said. Penny laughed.

"Why do you say that?" she asked. "Does it rattle?"

"Put your hand into the middle of the sheaf," said Tammylan. "Then you will feel how crisp and light and dry it is—and if you move your hand about you will hear a whispery, rattly noise. Yes—the corn's in rattling order!"

Tammylan and the farmer, followed by the four children, moved to other sheaves here and there in the field and felt to see if the corn was ready to be carted.

"We'll cart it tomorrow," said the farmer. "It is lovely weather—my word what a summer we've had!"

So the next day the wagons were sent into the cornfields to cart the corn away. Jim and Bill took their pitch-forks and threw the sheaves deftly into the wagons. It was good to watch them, for they worked easily and well. A sheaf was picked up by a fork, lifted and thrown into the wagon—then down it went again for another sheaf. Another man stood in the wagon to arrange the sheaves properly inside. If they were not stacked well there, the whole thing might topple over, once the cart began moving.

It was easy work as long as there was not much corn in the wagon—but as it got full, and the sheaves were built up higher and higher in the cart, Jim and Bill had to throw more strongly, right above their heads. Soon the wagon was groaning with the weight of the corn, which had been built up neatly in the cart, and was not likely to topple out.

"Come along, Benjy?" shouted Jim. "The wagon's ready. You can take it to the rick-yard."

Benjy and Rory ran to the horses harnessed to the loaded wagon. Sheila and Penny climbed up on to the load. It was not so soft as the hay had been, but was very pleasant to sit on as the creaking wagon rumbled slowly down the lanes.

The corn was pitched out of the wagon into the rick-yard, ready for the building of corn-stacks—then back to the cornfield went the two horses with the empty wagon. By that time the second wagon had been filled with corn-sheaves by the men, and Rory and Benjy had to un-harness the two horses and take the second wagon to the yard, leaving the first one in the field to be filled again.

It was glorious fun. Each time the girls rode home on the corn, high up in the air. Their mother saw them and smiled.

"Harvest home!" she said, when the last load was safely in. "Harvest home! Come along in—and you shall have a very special harvest-home supper, for I'm sure you are all hungry and thoroughly deserve it!"

So in they went—and the farm-hands went too, tired but happy because the harvest was in safely. What a lot they ate and drank, for they were all hungry and thirsty and tired!

The children fell asleep as soon as their heads touched their pillows that night. "It was the nicest day of the year," said Sheila to Penny, as she closed her eyes. "Harvest home! The very nicest day of all the year!"

CHAPTER XXII

SUMMER GOES BY

JIM and Bill built the corn into fine fat stacks. The children helped, of course! Nothing could go on in the farm without their help, Jim said!

It was fun to watch the men build the corn-stacks. They

first made the bottom of the stack, arranging the sheaves neatly in the right shape for the stack. Then Bill stood in the middle and caught the sheaves as Jim forked them to him. He stood them upright in a ring, but, as he worked to the outside, he stood them less and less upright till at the edge they were lying down.

Then Bill knelt down to his work, and he and Jim together soon had the corn-stack mounting higher and higher. "I suppose you children think you could build a stack easily enough?" called Bill.

"No," said Rory, doubtfully. "It looks rather difficult. You have to place the sheaves just so—the ends downwards at a certain slope—and Bill, do you know that you've got the centre of the stack higher than the outside edge?"

"Oh yes, I'm doing that on purpose," said Jim. "That's what's called keeping the heart full in a stack. If I don't do that, the rain will get in when the stack settles down."

Jim and Bill brought the head of the stack to a point, and tied the top sheaves firmly to one another.

"Is it finished now?" asked Penny.

"Oh no—it has to be thatched and roped," said Bill. "We'll not be finished for some time yet!"

Bill thatched the stack firmly, just as he had thatched the farmhouse itself. He began at the eaves of the stack and worked up to the top. He got Jim to hand him up water every now and again to damp the straw, for it was too dry to work with comfortably. He stroked the thatch down with a stick as he worked, and soon it began to look very neat indeed.

Then he and Jim roped the stack firmly. First they tied a rope round the body of the stack just below the eaves. Then they roped the thatched top firmly, running the rope round and round in a curious pattern and then tying it to the rope below the eaves.

"The stack looks simply lovely!" said Benjy, admiringly. "I'm sure the rain won't get into it."

"That it won't!" said Bill. "Now we'll get on to the next stack."

"Aren't you going to make your nice straw crown at the top of the stack?" asked Penny, disappointed.

"There's no time just now," said Bill. "I must start on the next stack—but when I've time to spare in the evenings I'll put my mark on each stack, Penny! Ah, you'll see golden crowns on the top of every one!"

Bill kept his word, and when the stacks were all finished, and stood solid and golden in the rick-yard Bill put his mark on them—a neat crown of twisted straw right at the very top of the stacks!

"I'd like to do that," said Penny. "It must be so nice to sign your name on a beautiful stack, like that!"

"I wouldn't put my mark on a stack unless I'd done it well," said Bill. He had trimmed his stacks with his shears and was really proud of them.

Sheila's hens were thrilled to be loose in the rick-yard after the stacks had been made. There was so much corn to peck at, so many grains to scratch for. They filled the air with contented clucks, and laid more eggs than ever.

"Good corn always makes hens lay well," said Fanny, as she counted the eggs and entered them in the egg-book.

Penny's three calves were big by now. They were in the field with the cows, and had a lovely time there, chasing one another and sometimes butting their little heads against the sides of the staid cows. They always came running when they saw Penny, and the little girl was very fond of them.

Skippetty had grown into a small sheep! He was no longer so frolicsome, but seemed to think himself rather important and grown-up. Jim said it would be better for him to go into the sheep-field now, so Penny sadly gave him up.

"It was so nice having him follow me about everywhere," she said. "He was such a darling when he was a skippetty lamb, feeding out of a bottle. Animals grow up far too quickly—much more quickly than children. Why, in a few months they have grown up—and yet it seems to me as if I've been little for ages and ages. Animals are lucky!"

"Don't you believe it!" said Tammylan. "It's good to be young for a long time. You can learn so much more!"

But the children didn't agree with that at all! They thought it would be nice to be like the animals and not have to do so many lessons.

Although Skippetty was now almost a sheep in his looks, he always looked out for Penny when she came by. Then he would bleat for joy and run to her, frisking round her in his old joyful way. Penny was glad that he had remembered her.

"But it makes me sad to think he will be so like the sheep next year that I shan't know him," she said to Davey. "I shall miss my dear little Skippetty then."

"No, you won't, Tuppenny," said Davey, comfortingly. "And do you know why?"

"No. Why?" asked Penny.

"Well, because you'll have more new-born lambs to look after!" said Davey, smiling at her. "I shall give you one or two to see to for me, because you are so good with them. So don't look sad and sigh for last spring and Skippetty—but look forward to next spring and new lambs to feed from a bottle!"

"Oh, I will!" said Penny, joyfully. "That's a good idea, Davey. It's much nicer to look forward than to look back!"

"That's the best of farm-life," said old Davey. "We're always looking forward—wondering what our crops are going to be like—hoping that our young creatures will do well—planning all kinds of things."

The four children loved the summer months, especially when the fruit was ripening. They helped to harvest the fruit crop, and Penny ate so many plums that she made herself quite ill for a day or two.

The apple harvest was the most important fruit crop for Willow Farm. The orchards had many fine apple trees, and these were bearing well, though not as well as they sometimes did.

"They bore marvellously last year," said Jim. "You don't often get fruit trees bearing wonderfully well for two years running. But you'll have plenty to eat, plenty to set by in the apple-loft for the winter, and plenty to sell!"

The children felt certain that they could manage the apple harvesting by themselves. The orchards were not very large, and as it was still holiday time, the boys said that they would like to spend a week in the apple trees, picking and storing the apples.

"We can help too," said Sheila, at once. "You boys can have the tree-climbing to do, and Penny and I will stay below and take the apples from you."

The farmer said that the four children could pick the fruit. "But remember this," he said. "The whole secret of having good clean fruit that keeps well and doesn't go bad is not to bruise it. Will you remember that? Handle the apples gently and if you drop any, put them on one side so that we may eat those first. I don't want to store any that are likely to go bad."

The children remembered his advice. The boys picked carefully, standing on the ladders, and putting the fruit into big baskets swung on the branches with hooks. When they were filled the girls took them down to the ground.

Sheila and Penny picked over the apples carefully. Any that were at all pecked by the birds or bitten by wasps they put on one side for Harriet to use in the near future. Any that they dropped they put on one side also.

"Now these are the quite perfect ones," said Sheila, looking at a pile of beautiful smooth red apples. "We must take them to the loft in baskets. Put them in very carefully,

Penny. Oh—you've dropped one, butter-fingers! That must go to the bruised pile!"

Soon the apple-loft was smelling very sweet indeed. The girls laid out the apples very carefully in long rows.

"Don't let them touch each other if you can help it, Penny," said Sheila. "If you do, one bad one will turn all the others rotten."

Their father came to see their work. He was very pleased. "My word, you are neat and tidy!" he said. "And how well you have picked out the apples! Not one pecked one among them! We shall be having apple-pie next May at this rate, for the apples will keep beautifully."

The children worked very hard at picking and storing the apples, and for payment they were allowed to have as many as they liked.

Penny ate so many that the others told her she would turn into an apple herself. "Your cheeks are already like two rosy apples," said Rory, solemnly. "You be careful, Penny."

Penny went to look in her mirror. She saw two plump cheeks, as red as the apples she had picked. "Oh goodness!" she said. "I really must be careful!"

So poor Penny didn't eat as many apples as before—but still, as Mother said, six or seven apples was quite enough for anyone, and that was the number that Penny still got through every day!

CHAPTER XXIII

GOOD LUCK FOR WILLOW FARM!

THE year went on. September came and lessons began again. All the crops had been gathered in and stored. The potatoes had been harvested, and the farmer was pleased with them. The mangold wurzels had not done so well, because so many of the seeds had not come up. But the farmer said that was quite usual with mangolds.

"We must get them in before the frosts come," he said, when the autumn came. So the big mangold wurzels were gathered and stored in pits, covered with earth and straw.

"The sheep and cattle will be glad of these in the winter," said Bill, as he stored the big roots in their pits. "The turnips will give them good eating too. I've stored them in a pit in the field. We've plenty for all the animals."

When the early days of December came a large machine arrived at Willow Farm. It was drawn by a traction engine which made an enormous noise coming up the narrow lanes.

"Whatever is it?" asked Rory.

"Oh good—it's the threshing-machine coming," said the farmer, pleased. "I hired it for the beginning of December, and here it is! It has come to thresh our corn and get the wheat for us!"

"Why didn't you borrow it from Uncle Tim?" asked Sheila.

"He hasn't got one," said her father. "Farmers don't usually own threshing-machines—it is easier and cheaper to hire them when we want them. They go from farm to farm. Now it is our turn to have it."

"But why do we want it?" asked Penny. "We've got our corn in!"

"Ah, but the grain has to be beaten from the ears!" said her father. "We can't eat it straight from the corn-stack, Penny—or would you like to try it?"

"No thank you," said Penny. "But we don't eat corn either, Daddy, do we? The hens do that."

"Well, we shall sell our corn to the miller," said her father. "He will grind it into flour—and we shall buy it to bake our bread and to make our cakes and puddings."

Soon the air was full of a deep, booming sound. "That's the thresher at work," said the farmer. "You can go and see it when you come back from school."

The children raced home from their lessons. They went to the rick-yard, where the corn-stacks stood, and there they saw the big threshing-machine. Nearby stood the traction-engine that had brought it, and that set it to work.

When Scamper heard the noise nearby he leapt from Benjy's shoulder and bounded into the bare trees. He was really frightened of it. Penny felt a little bit scared too, but she soon became brave enough to go near and see what was happening.

It was very interesting. Bill was up on a stack, forking out the sheaves that he had so carefully arranged there. He threw them to Jim, who quickly cut the bands that bound the sheaves together. Then he put the loose corn-stalks into the mill just below him—and they fell into a swiftly revolving drum in which were six long arms or "beaters" that struck the corn and beat out the grain from the ears.

The grain fell through into another kind of machine called a winnowing machine, where the chaff was blown away from the grain. Then the wheat fell out into sacks held ready by the farmer himself. He was pleased to see such yellow grain filling his sacks! As soon as one sack was full he heaved it away and put another empty one to be filled. Rory and Benjy helped him. It was great fun.

The straw tumbled out loose, and was stacked in a shed. "It will make fine bedding for the cattle in the winter," said Rory.

"Yes, and we'll chop it up and put it into their food too," said Jim. "There's not much wasted from the corn!"

"What about the chaff?" asked Sheila, as she watched the light chaff being put into sacks too.

"Ah, my wife will be along for some of that," said Bill. "Our mattresses are filled with chaff, you know—and we like good new chaff each year. We shall have fine bedding now!"

"Goodness!" said Benjy, "what a lot of good the corn is! Wheat for making flour—straw for animal bedding and for thatching—and chaff for mattresses!"

All that day and the next the threshing-mill boomed on the farm, as it worked in the rick-yard. Soon all the farmer's corn was turned into grain, straw and chaff, and the farmer and his men looked with pride at their full sacks.

"It's a good harvest," said the farmer, as he dipped his fingers into a full sack and let the grain trickle through them. "Our fields have done well this year."

When the threshing-mill had rumbled away again down the lanes, pulled by the heavy traction-engine, the weather changed from cold and sunny, to damp and grey. Rain-mists hid the countryside and the children could no longer go over the fields to their lessons. Instead they had to go down the lanes and along the main road. This was very much farther, and they had to start out earlier and get back later.

Penny was tired. Her legs were not so long as the others, and she didn't like trudging so far in bad weather. She was very glad when the Christmas holidays came and she had no longer to get up early and walk three miles to school.

"Do you think we had better send the children to boarding-school?" said their father one day. "They can't walk all that way all the winter through. Penny looks quite tired out. It's impossible to spare a horse and wagon four times a day. I almost think they had better go away to school."

But when the children heard this idea they were really horrified. "What!" cried Rory, "leave Willow Farm for nine months every year, just when things were beginning to be exciting! Oh Daddy, how can you think of such a thing!"

The four children were so worried about this idea that they went to tell Tammylan. It was five days before Christmas. They set out over the damp fields, and came to his cave. He had left his tree-house, of course, and was now living cosily in the cave. His friend the hare was, as usual, beside him.

"Hallo!" called the children, and ran to meet their friend. "How are you, Tammylan? We haven't seen you for ages."

Tammylan told them his news, and then he asked for theirs.

"Tammylan, we've bad news," said Rory. "Do you know Mummy and Daddy are actually thinking of sending us all away to boarding-school, because we have such a long way to walk to our lessons now that the winter has come and we can't go across the wet fields!"

"Oh, that would be dreadful!" said the wild man. "I should miss you all terribly."

"Tammylan, go and talk to Daddy and Mummy about it," said Penny, slipping her hand into Tammylan's. She thought the wild man could do anything. She could not bear the thought of leaving Willow Farm to go to school. What, leave the calves and Skippetty—and not be able to have new lambs to feed in the spring—and not see the new chicks and ducklings! It was too dreadful to think of!

"Well, I'm going over to Willow Farm tomorrow to take your father something," said Tammylan. "I'll have a word with him—but I don't think that anything I can say will make any difference! After all, it *is* a long way for you all to walk, especially little Penny."

The children were out Christmas shopping when Tammylan went over to the farm the next day, so they did not see him or hear if he had said anything to their parents. Indeed, they were so excited over their shopping that they even forgot to worry about going to school after the Christmas holidays!

"Can Tammylan come for Christmas Day?" asked Penny. "Do ask him, Mummy!"

"Oh, he's coming," said her mother. "He'll be along after breakfast."

Christmas Day dawned cold and sunny and bright. The children woke early and found their stockings full of exciting things. Even Rory and Sheila had stockings, for that was the one day of the year when they felt as childish as Penny and begged for stockings too!

Mummy had given them a watch each. Rory and Sheila had had watches before, but Rory had lost his and Sheila had broken hers. Now each child had a neat silver watch and they were overjoyed. They all strapped them proudly on their wrists.

They went down to the kitchen and gave presents to Harriet and Fanny. Fanny was delighted to have so many presents. Her face beamed with joy as she opened her parcels and found a smart pencil from Rory, a book from Sheila, a thimble from Benjy and some sweets from Penny.

"And thank you, Fanny, for being such a help with the hens," said Sheila. "Won't it be fun to have chicks again in the spring!"

The children left the kitchen and then Rory said something that had been in everyone's mind.

"How funny! Everyone has given us a present, except Daddy!"

Their father overheard him. He smiled.

"My present is coming along soon," he said. "I couldn't find room in your stockings for it! Watch out of the window and you'll see it arriving soon!"

The children squealed with joy and ran to the window. They simply could not imagine what their father was giving them.

But they soon found out! Tammylan appeared—but he was not alone! With him were four grey donkeys, plump and lively. The children could hardly believe their eyes.

"Daddy! Are the donkeys your present?" shouted Rory. "One for each of us?"

"Yes—one for each of you!" said his father with a smile. "Tammylan came along the other day and begged so hard for you to stay on at Willow Farm instead of going to school—and he suggested giving you a donkey each to ride over the fields, so that you might stay on here. Your mother and I thought it would be a splendid idea, and Tammylan said he would go to the market and buy the donkeys in time for Christmas. He knew someone who was selling six. So he chose four and here they are!"

The children tore out of the door and rushed to Tammylan! They were so pleased and excited that they could hardly wish him a happy Christmas!

"Which is my donkey?" cried Rory. "Oh, aren't they beauties!"

Tammylan gave each child a donkey. The two biggest went to the boys, and the other two to the girls. Each child mounted at once and galloped off round the farm. They were so happy that they sang as they went.

"Now we shan't have to leave Willow Farm, Willow

Farm, Willow Farm!" they all sang. "Gee-up, donkeys, gee-up! Oh, what a fine life you'll have here!"

The children's parents watched with Tammylan, laughing as they saw the happy children galloping all over the place.

When they came back at last, their father spoke to them. "You have all worked so well this year," he said. "You have been such a help. You haven't grumbled or complained, you have been cheerful and happy, and you have helped to make our farm a great success. So it is only fair that you should share in that success, and that is why I have spent part of the farm's money on each of you. What are you going to call your donkeys?"

"Mine shall be Neddy?" said Rory.

"Mine's Bray!" said Benjy.

"Mine's Canter!" said Sheila.

"And mine's Hee-Haw!" said Penny. And just as she said that her donkey threw up his head and brayed loudly. "He-haw! Hee-haw! Hee-haw!"

"There! He's saying his name to me!" said Penny, with a laugh. "Oh Daddy—what a lovely present! And to think we don't need to go away to school now! How lovely! Oh, what fun it will be to ride to lessons on four grey donkeys every morning and afternoon!"

And there we will leave them all, galloping in delight over the fields of Willow Farm. "Our dear, dear farm!" said Penny. "Oh, I wonder what will happen next year—there's always something exciting on a farm. I'm sure next year will be greater fun than ever!"

But that, of course, is another story.

says...

'Yo-ho-ho for your next book from the Armada ship! There's a cargo of exciting reading for you—so set sail with another Armada book now.

You'll find more titles listed over the page.'

The Hardy Boys Adventure Stories

by Franklin W. Dixon

The escapades of Frank and Joe Hardy, sons of a famous detective, and their staunch friend, Chet Morton, lead to breathtaking dangers and adventures. If you can't resist a gripping plot, daring heroes, death-dealing villains, hair's-breadth escapes and plenty of action, the Hardy Boys are for you!

The Mystery of the Aztec Warrior
The Arctic Patrol Mystery
The Haunted Fort
The Mystery of the Whale Tattoo
The Mystery of the Disappearing Floor
The Mystery of the Desert Giant
The Mystery of the Melted Coins
The Mystery of the Spiral Bridge
The Clue of the Screeching Owl
The Twisted Claw
The Sign of the Crooked Arrow
The Clue in the Embers
What Happened at Midnight
The Sinister Signpost
Footprints Under the Window
The Crisscross Shadow

Watch out for more Hardy Boys adventures.

Have you read all these books by Judith Berrisford in Armada?

JACKIE WON A PONY

The wonderful story of how Jackie wins Misty – the pony she has always longed for.

TEN PONIES AND JACKIE

Jackie and her friends start up a riding stable. And despite some near-fatal disasters, the Christmas holidays end in a resounding success.

JACKIE'S PONY PATROL

When Jackie and Babs plan a holiday in the Pony Forest, they find themselves involved in a thrilling adventure – chasing a gang of thieves.

JACKIE AND THE PONY TREKKERS

Pony trekking in Wales for Jackie and Babs. But it's not the relaxing summer they expected . . .

JACKIE'S PONY CAMP SUMMER

Living under canvas, Jackie and Babs become involved in a bitter feud that nearly spells disaster for Misty.

JACKIE AND THE PONY BOYS

Why do the three show-jumping boys hate Jackie and her friends? The pony boy 'war' leads to accidents – and, worse still, a fearful quarrel between Jackie and Babs . . .

JACKIE'S SHOW JUMPING SURPRISE

Alone at Stableways, Jackie must ride to save the day – on a Grand National winner . . !